LONESOME END

STEPHEN W. MEADER

Lonesome End

Illustrated by Ned Butterfield

Dedication

The republication of this book is dedicated with love to Chester Storthz---All-American running back, songwriter, poet, creative genius who teaches me the meaning of loyalty and trust every day---by his best friend, Jerry Atchley.

LONESOME END

1

Nobody paid much attention to the lanky sixteen-year-old who rode up the main street of Gunstock, Kansas, that Saturday morning. Tod Ross didn't mind. He was used to being alone a lot and was perfectly able to take care of himself. The less other people bothered him, the better.

His face was sober, almost stern, in spite of its youthful lines, and he was tanned by sun and prairie wind. He wore a weather beaten Stetson, faded, work-stained jeans, and an ancient pair of boots, run over at the heels. His long legs hung down on either side of his buckskin pony. Big hands, on the end of rawboned wrists, rested on the saddle pommel, holding the reins loosely.

Gunstock wasn't much of a place, but on this one occasion it swarmed with cars and people. This was Rodeo Day—the town's day of glory—and strangers had come in from a long distance around. Tod himself had ridden thirty miles since sunup. But unlike the others, he wasn't there as a spectator. What he wanted was to make a very special purchase, and in order to do it, he had to win some money in the calf-roping contest.

Parked cars filled every space along the curb, but Tod finally found a three-foot hole beside a Volkswagen and

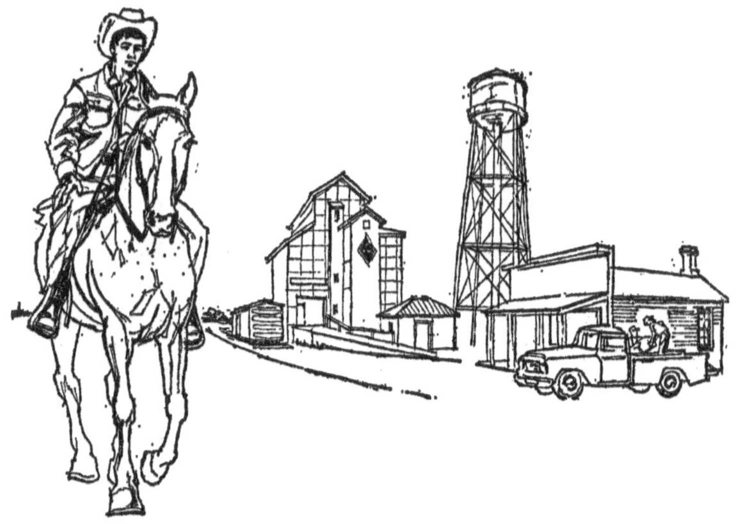

hitched his pony to the rail that still remained there at the edge of the sidewalk, a relic of older times. Pushing his way through the crowds, he watched the store fronts till he came to one that had a huge poster in the window.

"Gunstock Rodeo Headquarters," it announced. "Saturday, Sept. 3. Big cash prizes! All entries must be in before 12 noon. Entry fee, $10 for each event."

The time on the wall clock inside was now ten-fifty, and Tod found half a dozen men clustered in front of the desk. Some were regular rodeo riders, leathery-faced and whipcord-tough. Others were no older than himself—ranch boys hoping to win fame and earn some spending money.

After a brief wait he finally stood at the desk and caught the attention of a harried-looking man seated behind it.

"All right, sonny." The clerk sighed. "You want to enter? It'll cost you ten bucks, 'case you didn't know it."

"Calf roping," Tod told him. "Here's the money. Name's Tod Ross, from Prairie, Kansas."

He fished crumpled bills from the tight pocket of his jeans

10

and laid them on the desk. The clerk wrote the name on his list and handed Tod a receipt.

"Give that to the fellow at the pens," he said. "Next!"

Tod folded the paper carefully and put it in his shirt pocket. Outside, he turned his steps toward the saddlery and outfitting store on the next corner. At the moment there were no other customers. A dapper salesman looked the tall ranch boy over, yawned, and languidly asked if there was anything he wanted.

"Yep," said Tod. "I'd like to see a pair o' boots. Good ones."

The man gave him another supercilious glance. "Step this way," he said with a wave of his hand. "Work boots are right over here. We're having a special sale, you know—nine ninety-five."

"Nope," Tod told him. "Work boots aren't what I want. These are more like it." And he pointed to a pair of elegant Texas boots with embossed leather tops.

"But," the salesman told him with a frown, "those are fifty dollars a pair! Even marked down for the sale, they're forty-two fifty. I—er—wonder if you can afford them."

"What I want," said Tod, "is to try 'em on for size. If you've got a pair that fits, you can save 'em for me. I'll come in an' pay for 'em later this afternoon."

Reluctantly the man measured his foot for size and brought a pair of the fancy boots from the shelf. Tod pulled them on, walked a few steps, and reveled in their soft comfort.

"These'll do fine," he said. "Like I told you, I'll be back for 'em. So don't sell 'em."

A moment later he was riding down Main Street toward the Fair Grounds, where the rodeo would take place. The weathered grandstand was already beginning to fill up. On beyond were the stock barns and corrals, and it was toward them that Tod guided the buckskin.

11

There was a lot of activity around the pens. Contestants were looking over the animals they would have to work with, and their cowboy friends were giving them humorous advice. Tod watered his horse and tied him to the fence. Then he got a feed bag from behind his saddle and doled out a sparing ration of oats.

"I know you think that's a pretty puny feed, Buck," he told the pony amiably. "But you've got to stay sharp for later on."

He had also brought along a sandwich for himself, and this he proceeded to eat, washing it down with a bottle of pop. It was while he was chewing on the last mouthful that a deep voice spoke at his elbow.

"Hi, there, Ross," it said. "Long ways from home, ain't you? What you doin' so far from Prairie High? Just here to watch, or are you ridin'?"

Looking around, Tod recognized the big fellow as Mike Hoban, a year ahead of him at school and a tackle on the football team.

"Hi!" he replied with a grin. "I aim to rope me a calf. Reckon you're in the bronc riding, aren't you?"

"That's right. Have you checked in an' drawn your number?"

"Not yet," Tod replied. "I was just getting ready to."

Together they walked to the outdoor table where a sign announced "Calf Roping." A man in a ten-gallon hat took Tod's entry receipt and wrote down his name.

"Here," he said, holding out another hat. "Put your hand in without lookin' an' draw yourself a card."

The grimy piece of green pasteboard Tod pulled out bore the number nine.

Hoban nodded his approval. "Good," he said. "You'll have time to see how the others do. Me, I'd rather have a high number any time. But I'm ridin' third in the bareback, an' I drew a second in the steer wrestling."

12

Tod looked at his companion's husky frame. They were about the same height, but Hoban must have outweighed him by fifty pounds.

"With your build," he said, "I can see why you go in for bulldogging steers. But what about saddle broncs? Don't you like to ride 'em?"

"They're generally tougher than the bareback mounts," Mike explained. "An' I got my foot caught in the stirrup once. After that I stuck to horses I could get off of easier."

He chuckled at the recollection. "Ever been in a rodeo before?" he asked.

"Nope," Tod replied. "But I've seen a few. An' I've been roping an' branding calves since I was ten. I'm not too scared to try."

"Attaboy!" His friend laughed. "I'll be pullin' for you!"

There was an hour to wait before the events got under way, and the two boys spent the time wandering around the corrals. Mike, of course, was most interested in the stock to be used for the bareback riding, which would come first on the program.

"Don't any of 'em look too mean," he commented. "I can tell better when I climb aboard in the chute. Hope I get one that'll give me a good rough ride, though—for points."

The calves were a mixed lot, some scrawny and underfed, others with the blocky build of Herefords. But all of them looked scared and nervous. About the best Tod could hope for was that the one he drew would run in a straight line.

At one o'clock a bugle blared out the signal for the riders to take their places at the chutes.

"So long, Mike," said Tod, "an' lots o' luck. I'll be watching you."

He saw the big lad settle his hat firmly and stride away. Then he found a spot high on the corral fence, where he could see everything that happened in the arena.

The first rider was a wiry little cowhand from the Gunstock area, and a big hand went up for him from the stands when his name came over the loudspeaker. Before the cheers had died, the chute gate opened and a rough-haired black horse came charging out. The rider beat the air with his right hand and spurred his mount's flanks bravely, but at the first real buck he lost his balance and pitched forward over the horse's head. He was lying flat on the ground when the eight-second buzzer went off. Of course, there was no score.

Next came a professional rodeo rider, a man of thirty or more, with a hard-bitten face and a gaudy western shirt. His bronco acted mild enough till he was well clear of the gate. Then it began to buck viciously and twist sidewise in midair. The man sat erect, his left hand gripping the hackamore rope, his heels raking the horse's side. He stayed on through half a dozen of those leaps and lunges before the buzzer announced the end of the ride. When he had been pulled off, Tod saw that he walked with a limp. Like so many rodeo riders, he had probably been smashed up half a dozen times, but he knew his business. After a moment the judges' score was called out, and it was a good one. "That ride gives him a seventy-three!" intoned the man at the microphone.

It would be Mike Hoban's turn now, and Tod hunched forward tensely, watching the chute. He didn't exactly pray, but he hoped hard that his friend had drawn a horse that would give him a good ride.

When the gate flew open, he saw it—a big, hammer-headed bay with four white stockings. "Mike Hoban, of Prairie," the announcer chanted, "on Moocher, out o' Gate Three."

Tod needn't have worried about the performance Moocher would give. The horse arched its back high and went up, all four feet together. Mike, who had come out stylishly, with both heels as high as the bronco's withers, took the

14

jarring jolt of the descent, then fanned the air with his free hand and jammed his spurs into the dusty flanks.

"Ride him, Mike!" Tod heard himself yelling. And the bay horse sunfished, twisting in mid-leap. Mike hung onto the rope, but daylight was visible between him and the horse's back. By luck and skill he came down into position without being thrown. Again and again the bay bucked furiously while the slow seconds ticked by. Then the buzzer sounded its call, and a rider galloped up to pull Mike off. The people in the stands had liked the ride and were yelling their approval, but all Tod wanted to hear was the score. It seemed a long time coming.

At last the loudspeaker bellowed the words. "A nice ride by young Mike Hoban," said the announcer. "He made a score of—seventy-two!"

Tod left the fence to go and meet his schoolmate. He thought Mike might be a little disappointed, but the big lad was smiling broadly.

"How 'bout that?" he asked. "First time I ever got more'n a sixty or sixty-five! Ol' Moocher sure did a job, didn't he?"

The next contestant was already making his ride while they talked, but a lazy horse produced a score well below the leaders'. Then came two unlucky riders who were thrown almost before they started. And the seventh and last man in the event scored only sixty-seven for third place.

"Well," said Mike, "second money's better'n I'd figured. Reckon I'll go collect it. But you'd better get ready for the calf ropin'. That comes next."

Tod found his pony looking rested and alert. He tightened the cinch, then took his rope off the saddle and shook out a running loop. It was a good rope, used enough to be smooth-handling, but still stout. Out of the saddlebag he took a "pigging string"—the yard-long piece of cord that was used to hog-tie the calf. This he would hold in his teeth when the time came. Buck eyed these preparations expectantly. He gave a little snort and pawed the ground with a forefoot.

"Not yet, boy," Tod told the eager horse. "Nothing to do right now but wait."

Buck was twelve years old now and couldn't be expected to win many races against younger mounts. But he was wise and quick—a first-class cutting and roping horse. As Tod's father, Big James Ross, had often said, "Buck's got cow sense." He meant that the pony knew which way a steer or a calf was going to jump and could move fast enough to beat the animal to it.

The call for the calf ropers came over the loudspeaker, and giving his pony a pat on the nose, Tod went back to the rail to watch. This was largely a boys' event, with only two or three older men competing. The first lad to leave the barrier was on a beautiful palomino quarter horse that sprinted out like a deer. In fact, he was so fast that he overran the frightened calf before his rider could throw the loop. Reining in, he came back and roped the calf on the second try. But his time, after tying the animal's legs, was an ignominious twenty-two seconds.

Those who followed did better. After the fourth roper finished his throw and tie, the time was announced as twelve and four-fifths. Tod began to feel butterflies in his stomach, so he went back and swung into the saddle. He rubbed his sweating hands on his jeans and rode over to the pens, where he found Mike Hoban waiting for him.

"Nothing to it, boy!" Mike told him with a grin. "If you get a good calf, I bet you can beat those other cowpokes easy!"

Tod didn't have an answer. He looked over the calves that remained in the pen and wondered which one would be number nine. They all looked tall and rangy now that the time drew near.

The seventh contestant was waiting his turn now. The

16

gate opened, and a little brindled calf dashed out, the rider following as soon as the barrier fell. He was spinning a fine loop, but the calf ran in zigzags so that the first cast missed.

"Too bad!" Mike said. "He's in bad trouble now."

The second try succeeded, and the rider made a good tie, but his time was over twenty seconds.

Only one more to go now. The eighth roper was a grown man on a good-looking horse that seemed fidgety. "He'd better watch that pony," Tod thought to himself. And sure enough, the instant the calf was released, the horse broke through the barrier too soon.

"Disqualified!" yelled the announcer. "Final contestant in this event is Tod Ross, from Prairie."

Tod gulped and rode Buck into position. It had taken a minute or two to fix the barrier tape where it had been broken. Now all was ready. A glance into the chute beside him showed Tod a big calf—one of those chunky white-faces.

Then the gate flew open, and the Hereford was running. Buck had gathered his feet under him, and the instant the barrier dropped, he darted in pursuit. Feeling cool now, Tod made his loop and saw the calf heading straight out across the arena. One quick cast and the noose settled over its head, while Buck braced his feet to pull the rope taut. Even before the horse stopped, Tod had flung himself out of the saddle and was running. At the jerk of the rope, the calf turned a somersault, and as it struggled to get up, Tod slid an arm over its back to grab the opposite foreleg. Then he heaved with all his might. The stocky calf came reluctantly, but come it did, falling with a solid thud on its back and side. Tod caught three of the feet together, whipped the pigging string around them twice—three times—and made his tie. Then, all in the same motion, he rose, flinging up his hands.

Through the pound of blood in his ears, he could hear a

lot of cheering. Then, as a judge checked the firmness of the tie and signaled the stand that it held, the announcer came on the air, startlingly loud. "Time," he roared, "nine and two-fifths seconds. That's a record for this rodeo, and it wins for young Mr. Ross!"

2

Still in a daze, Tod coiled his rope and led the buckskin pony back through the gate, where Mike Hoban was waiting. The big youngster greeted him with a bear hug.

"Man!" he cried. "That was some ropin'! First money! I bet your pa'll be proud!"

"Pa doesn't know I'm here," said Tod. "All I told him was I had to go an' buy a pair o' boots. What time is it? Do you know?"

" 'Round two-thirty, I guess. The saddle broncs come next, an' the steer wrestlin' won't be on till close to four o'clock."

"Gee!" said Tod with real regret. "I won't be able to watch you then. I reckon you've got a car, but I have to ride old Buck home, an' I don't want to push him too hard. Good luck, anyhow! I'll see you at school."

He got his fifty dollars first prize money and rode soberly back to the outfitting store. The clerk looked somewhat surprised to see him, but after staring at the money in the boy's hand, he produced the beautiful boots.

"I'll wear em," said Tod, handing over the bills. "Wrap these old ones up for me, please."

It wasn't until he stood proudly in the new boots that

the salesman found breath to ask a question. "You—you mean you won the money at the rodeo?" he asked.

"Well," Tod told him with a grin, "I didn't rob a bank, if that's what you mean."

Some time after five o'clock, his pony was plodding down the shoulder of the road, more than halfway home. The setting sun was in Tod's eyes, and the never-ceasing prairie wind blew dust that settled on his clothes. Wheat field and cattle range, the brown plains of Kansas stretched away to the horizon.

Many cars had passed before he heard a squeal of brakes and a honking horn. A Chevy pickup truck came to a stop beside him.

"How you doin', Tod?" Mike Hoban called from the cab.

"Fair enough. How'd you make out with the steers?"

"Took a third," the big boy replied happily. "Made it quite a day. I wish I could give you a lift, but I reckon your pony wouldn't fit too good in this thing."

"Thanks," Tod called, "but we'll get on fine. So long, now!"

He looked after the rapidly disappearing truck and patted Buck's neck. "Come on, boy," he said. "You aren't that tired." And the horse responded by breaking into an easy canter.

Tod wished he could have watched the steer wrestling. He was glad Mike had done so well. In his years at school, he had never made any close friends, but he felt as if Mike Hoban and he had a common bond.

It was nearly dark when he reached the home ranch. He fed and stabled his horse, then went in by the kitchen door. Big Jim Ross sat there at the table with a cup of coffee.

"Where you been, son?" he asked gruffly.

"I rode to Gunstock," said Tod. "Bought me a new pair o' boots."

"So? An' where'd you get that much cash? I didn't give it to you."

Tod braced himself. "I won the calf-roping contest at the rodeo."

His father's stern face relaxed, and he broke into a chuckle. "Ol' Buck took you all the way up there an' then won top money? What was your time?"

"Nine an' two-fifths, I guess it was. They're real nice boots, Pa. Look at 'em."

"OK, Tod, I reckon you earned 'em. Come on—wash up an' eat your supper."

*　*　*

Tod was wearing the fancy boots when he entered his new homeroom at Prairie High School on Monday morning, the first day of the fall term. He was a junior now, one of about twenty boys in his class. There were a few more girls than boys, but as far as he was concerned, girls didn't count. The homeroom teacher was "Dutch" Kleinschmidt, who not only taught chemistry but also coached football and baseball. He was probably the most popular member of the faculty.

They were seated alphabetically, with Tod between a lad named Joe Peters and one called "Finny" Smith. Directly behind him sat three that he knew somewhat better—Ricardo Villa, a Mexican, inevitably called "Pancho," Andy Willis, a young Negro, and the storekeeper's son, Aaron Weil. All three of them were on the football squad.

"Hey, Ross," Willis whispered as the class was settling, "I hear you showed 'em how, up at Gunstock!"

Tod shrugged. "Just got a lucky calf," he answered with a smile.

No more compliments were paid him until after lunch, when some of the boys were playing touch football out on the field. There were no teams, and anybody could get in who

22

wanted. Tod was watching on the sideline when he suddenly heard his name shouted.

"Take it, Ross!"

A spiral pass was sailing toward him out of nowhere, and he put up a big hand, caught it, and started running. The new boots felt light and speedy. He outsprinted the nearest boy, dodged the second, and deposited the ball beyond the goal line.

"What did I tell yuh?" a deep voice called. "He's a natural! Just look at those meathooks! An' he's fast, too!"

Looking about in puzzlement, Tod saw Mike Hoban pointing at him while everyone else stared. Somewhat confused by all the attention, he walked back to the school building. Having people cheer when he won the calf roping was reasonable enough, but this seemed to him ridiculous. He went to his homeroom and opened a history book to do some studying.

Mr. Kleinschmidt came in a moment later and found him there alone.

"Ever play any football, Ross?" he asked pleasantly.

"No, sir," said Tod. "Not really—just fooling around with a ball."

"That was a nice catch you made out there. And when you had it, you seemed to know what to do with it. We'll be starting practice tomorrow. Why don't you try out for the team?"

"Gee, I never thought about it," Tod told him truthfully. "Our ranch is five miles out o' town, an' I have chores to do. Just figured I'd never have time for football."

"Well," the coach said, "I wish you'd think about it. We've got such a small squad, we need every player we can find. And one place we're weak is at right end. All we've got is Andy Willis, over at the left. The middle of the line is solid enough, and the backs are good—especially Flick Davis at quarter. He'd be a star passer if he had more than one receiver he could depend on."

Tod stared back at him. "You really think I could help?" he asked. "I'm 'most scared to ask my dad. He thinks games are a waste o' time, an' he wouldn't like it if my work didn't get done. The bus leaves right after school, too, so I'd have trouble getting home after practice."

Kleinschmidt smiled. "I can see some difficulties," he said, "but if you have the stuff to make a good end, it might even help us win a championship. Don't tell anybody I said that. All I meant was we might win a few games. Maybe I can work something out that'll make it easier for you."

The bell rang, and the rest of the students came trooping in. Tod tried to put the matter out of his mind. It wasn't as easy as he expected. All through his afternoon classes, his thoughts kept straying to football.

Secretly he had envied the boys on the squad ever since he had seen his first game as a freshman. The bruising drive of the linemen in scrimmage and the thrill of good down-field blocking and tackling made his pulse beat faster. More than anything else, Tod liked bodily contact—things like throwing a calf, or handling a fractious horse, or wrestling with the cowhands in the bunkhouse.

At three-thirty, when he strapped up his books and went out to board the bus, Mike Hoban was waiting for him.

"I've got the pickup," Mike told him. "I'll give you a ride home. Want to talk to you."

The Hoban place was a mile or two beyond Tod's home, so he knew it wasn't out of his friend's way. He got in without argument.

"I generally drive, this time o' year," said Mike. "Even after football practice I can get home less'n an hour after the bus. Be glad to take you every day if you decide to come out for the team."

"Hey—hold on!" Tod laughed. "You must ha' been talking to Dutch Kleinschmidt."

"I did have a few words with him," Mike admitted. "He

24

was out at the field when I got Flick to throw you that pass. All of us were waitin' to see how you'd handle it. An' you did such a job, we knew you had somethin'."

"What's the matter with the pass-catchers you've got now?" Tod asked defensively.

"Well, at left end we're in pretty good shape. That little Negro boy, Andy Willis, doesn't catch 'em all the time, but when he gets one, he can sure scoot. It's Rudy Ryker, the right end, that's the problem. He's a nice guy, an' tall enough, but he's awkward. Can't seem to hang onto the football. If we could spare anybody else for right end, we might make a lineman out of him. I guess you know there aren't enough on the squad to give us two teams, so most of us have to play both ways—offense an' defense. If anybody gets hurt, we're in a real jam."

He drove on in silence for some distance, while Tod thought about what he had said.

"OK," said the younger boy at last. "I'd like to give it a try. All depends on Pa. If he puts his foot down, as he may, I'm sunk."

"Yippee!" cried his friend. "I'll see you out for practice tomorrow! That's how sure I am you can convince your father."

It didn't turn out to be easy, but after Tod had given him all the arguments he could think of, Jim Ross grudgingly gave in.

"Any time I find your chores aren't gettin' done or your grades are slippin'," he growled, "the deal's off. Maybe you'll get fed up with football after a week or so. I think it's a fool game anyhow."

So, feeling a bit sheepish, Tod went to the gym with Mike the next afternoon. He was assigned a locker and handed a uniform that almost fitted him. Like the others it was a brown-and-white jersey, patched and darned but clean; white stockings with brown stripes; tan pants; and ancient felt shoulder pads. The Prairie "Cowboys," as the team was called, had barely enough suits to go around, and there was no change for home or away games. A battered helmet was also issued to the new recruit, but the only shoes available were half a size too big. He tried them on but found them sloppy and clumsy.

"Reckon I can do better in my regular boots," he told Mike Hoban. "Anyhow, I know I can run faster."

The big lineman shook his head. "Too bad!" he said. "Such pretty boots, too. They'll be cut an' beat up after one hard scrimmage. I'll try an' find you a pair o' football shoes that fit better. Come on, now. Coach is waitin'!"

*　*　*

That first practice of the season was rough, for Dutch Kleinschmidt didn't spare the horses. Some of the town boys were soft and overweight, and he ran them up and down the field till the sweat poured off them. Then he called for tackling the dummy and falling on a loose ball. And finally he chose up two teams to scrimmage. Only the simplest running plays were used, but there were some bruises and a lot of tired muscles when it was over.

Tod came off better than some, for he was hardened by the summer's work. Still he was glad when the practice broke up. He took a quick shower, dressed, and was in the truck before five o'clock.

"How do you feel?" Mike asked. "Sort o' black an' blue? You did all right, Tod. That tackle when you busted up the end sweep was a honey."

"Who's on the first team?" Tod asked. "The way he mixed us all up, I couldn't tell."

"Well," Mike told him, "we only lost three men by graduation, so most o' the gang have played together for a couple o' years. I'd say the backfield was set—Flick Davis at quar-

26

ter, Joe Luke, the Cherokee, an' Tony Fortunato at the halves, an' Aaron Weil at fullback. In the line, starting at left end, there's Andy Willis, Chris Olsen, an' Wid Monroe. Link Carey plays center, an' he's a good one. Then comes Pancho Villa an' myself. All that's left is the right end —maybe Rudy Ryker. I hope by the time we play our first game, it'll be you."

His words troubled Tod somewhat. He had known the Ryker boy ever since they were in fourth grade. Rudy had always been bigger than the others in his class, but he had never bullied them. In fact, he was so good-natured that some of the smaller boys had picked on him. In sports, as in the classroom, he tried hard, but he never seemed to learn coordination.

Tod could understand why they had tried to make a football end out of Rudy, for he was over six feet tall and strong as an ox. Taking the position away from him would be no fun at all. And yet he knew, for the good of the team, he had to make the effort.

Mike pulled up by the Ross mailbox, and Tod got out. "Thanks for the ride," he said. "I can't hang around—got my chores to do. But I'll be seeing you tomorrow."

It was five minutes after five by the kitchen clock. He changed to his old work boots and hurried out to the barn. The ranch wasn't a very big one—only about two thousand acres—but they raised good Hereford steers and grew enough corn to fatten them.

One of the hands was in the barn, tinkering with the tractor. "Your paw's out in the west section, mendin' fence," he told Tod. "Said you was to saddle up an' ride out there."

The boy whistled up Buck in the corral and threw a saddle on him. Ten minutes later he spotted his father's horse standing at the edge of a little draw. Jim Ross was down in the ravine.

"Well," he growled, "I wondered when you'd get here. If you aren't too tired out playin' games, come fix this fence. Couple o' yearlin's broke out, an' I had to go round 'em up. Here's your tools."

3

Tod liked most jobs around the ranch, but fence-mending was a task nobody enjoyed. The break was naturally at the very bottom of the draw. The dip in the fence seemed to pull up the lowest stake, especially if the wire was stretched tight.

As his father rode away, he tamped the ground where the fencepost had been, then picked a new spot a few inches away and drove the stake down firmly with the sledge. Instead of using the stretcher to pull the wire taut, he did it with his gloved hand, then hammered in the staples that held it in place. Now, he figured, if a steer pushed against the wire, it would give a little without uprooting the post.

At supper his father unbent enough to ask about football practice. "Think you're goin' to be on the team?" he inquired.

"I guess so. May not get to be in there all the time, but they're so short o' players, I reckon they'll want to use me."

Mrs. McDonald, the housekeeper, spoke up from the stove. " 'Course they will!" she remarked loyally.

"Humph!" said Jim Ross. "Don't sound as if Prairie is likely to win many games!"

"We'll have to wait an' see," Told told him. "I wouldn't want to bet against us."

The word "us" came naturally o{}^{~} his tongue, and when he realized he had used it, he felt a ʌgle of pride.

*   *   *

By the end of the week, the squad had begun to work on some plays. Tod had a good memory, and he learned the signals without trouble. But more often than not, he scrimmaged on the scrub team and had to guess what the varsity would call in the huddle.

Mike Hoban had been right about the Texas boots. They were getting scratched up, and it was a relief when a decent pair of football shoes was found for him. Not quite so light as the boots, they did have cleats that helped him keep his footing. And after a few days' wear, he felt completely at home in them.

During the second week of practice, the coach had several of the boys throwing and catching passes on the sidelines. Tod and Rudy Ryker started from an imaginary scrimmage line and ran downfield, while the quarterback threw the ball to one or the other.

Tod had no difficulty at all. He simply reached up those big hands and clutched the ball instinctively. If it wasn't coming directly toward him—and Flick seemed to enjoy pitching wild ones—he shifted as far as necessary and grabbed it.

Ryker had more trouble. "Back, Rudy! Back!" Tod would yell at him, but the ball still sailed over his head.

Kleinschmidt watched but said nothing. The next day he called for regular scrimmage, and to nobody's surprise he put Ryker in at tackle on the scrub line, promoting Tod to right end on the first team. A couple of determined scrub defensive backs set out to break up Tod's pass receiving. They even double-teamed him on some plays, and it was obvious that they were following the coach's orders.

The toughened defense made it harder but more fun for

30

Tod. He quickly learned to run straight at the men in his way, then cut to right or left at the last second and depend on the quarterback to get the ball to him. When the scrub backs split, to foil him either way he turned, he simply put on speed, ran between them, and caught the ball well beyond the defenders. The safety man made a futile dive at his legs, but Tod sidestepped and went on to score.

The coach called him aside after practice. "Ross," he said, "you still have a lot to learn, but it'll come with some real game experience. I'm going to start you next week, when we play Wykoff. One thing we've got to find out is how you'll do on defense. Flick'll work with you on some pass patterns, but most of the time in scrimmage, I'm going to play you on the second team while the regulars run the ball."

Tod didn't mind the defensive work. It gave him a chance to shake off blockers and make some good hard tackles. He weighed only a little over a hundred and fifty pounds, despite his height of five-feet-eleven. But when he charged, he was like a terrier after a rat, and once he got those big hands on the man with the ball, he didn't let go.

Once, when he got up after a tackle, he caught a glimpse of a satisfied smile on Dutch Kleinschmidt's face. However, the coach gave him no words of praise. Instead, he was quick to point out mistakes—Tod's as well as others'.

The stiffness and bruises he had felt after the first week's practice were gone now. He felt tired but comfortably fit as he showered and dressed.

"Gettin' to like it, aren't you?" Mike Hoban asked him.

"Yep," said Tod. "I'll be glad when we play some real games, though."

Mike laughed as he steered the pickup out of the school-yard. "Yeah, I know it's more fun," he agreed. "But it isn't as easy. You'll be up against guys that know how to play an' want to win as much as you do. An' any mistake you make really hurts. We start off against the Wykoff Wildcats,

an' I know they're tough. They beat us twenty to nothin'
last year!"

"Maybe they won't be as good this time," Tod said hope-
fully, but Mike shook his head.

"They've got just about all their first team back," he re-
plied. "They'll outweigh us six or eight pounds to the man.
Just the same, I reckon we'll give 'em all the fight they want.
One thing—we'll be playin' on our home field."

Tod's father still grumbled at his getting home so late,
but once in a while he asked a question about the football
squad and its progress.

"When's the first game?" he inquired.

"Next week, Saturday—the twenty-third. Why, Pa? You
planning to come?"

"Not me!" The cattleman snorted. "Right in the middle
o' the fall round-up? I'll be too busy, an' you ought to know
it."

"Well, maybe you wouldn't think much o' the game anyhow," said Tod. "I've got a lot to learn before I'm any good,
an' they say Wykoff's going to outclass us."

"Who says? If that's the way you boys look at it, Prairie
deserves to get licked!"

Tod grinned but said no more. His father's interest was
greater than he had hoped.

*   *   *

The coach worked them harder than ever that final week.
Tod spent about half his time running the pass patterns
that Flick Davis taught him. But in scrimmage the emphasis
was on defense.

"You an' I," Mike Hoban told him, "have got to take out
the blockers on any play that comes our way. End sweeps
are up to you. If you can bust up the interference, one of
our linebackers'll get the ballcarrier, maybe even for a loss."

When the scrub team was unable to advance, Dutch

32

Kleinschmidt sometimes got into their line himself. Tod saw him pull out to lead the blockers, and the play was coming straight for his own position. Half afraid, he drove in to spill the coach. The next second he was on his back, gasping for breath, with his wind knocked out. And the second team had made a first down.

"Here," said Dutch, picking him up, "you came in too high. Get your shoulder down and smack it into the blocker's middle. Or if there are two of 'em, throw your body sidewise across their legs. Now we'll try it again."

Tod had his wind back and his dander up. This time he charged lower, and as he crashed into the coach, it knocked both of them down. The play fizzled after a two-yard gain.

"Good!" said Kleinschmidt. "That's the way to do it." And Tod was happy to see that he, too, was panting.

Most of the time the coach mixed the two teams, giving them about equal strength, and first-down yardage came harder.

"Wykoff isn't known as a passing team," he told them. "What we have to do is try to stop their ground game. Then, if they have to pass, maybe we can pick off one or two."

By Thursday night, the Cowboy squad was bone-tired but happy. They knew most of their rough edges had been rubbed off. Also there would be no scrimmage on Friday.

"It'll give you a chance to rest and polish up on your signals," the coach told them.

Saturday morning dawned hot and dry. Little gusts of wind blew dust devils across the prairie when Mike Hoban stopped for Tod shortly after noon. Both of them had eaten a light, early lunch.

"How do you feel?" Mike asked.

"Scared, I guess," Tod answered, and his friend chuckled.

"I know the feelin'," he said. "Little bugs jumpin' around in your stomach. That'll last till after the kickoff. Then, the first time you belt one o' the enemy, it all goes away."

There was still an hour to game time when they reached the gymnasium. Thanks to the girls in home economics class, their jerseys had been washed, dried, and mended on Friday, so that the squad looked fairly presentable when they were suited up.

"I don't have to tell you to do your best," said the coach. "Just remember these Wykoff boys aren't really wildcats at all. They're just as scared, and they get hurt just as easy as any other bunch of high-school kids. Trot out there now and run through a few plays, so you'll get loosened up. No fancy stuff, Flick. Just straight bucks and off-tackle plays. You know the starting lineup. I'm putting Ryker in at right end, and you'll stay on the bench a while, Ross."

Tod was disappointed, but he jogged out with the others, to the concerted cheering of the Prairie student body.

"Yea, Cowboys! Yea, COWBOYS!" they yelled. Tod's classmate, Mary Ann Foster, was the head cheerleader, and she looked pretty nice, he thought, in her short skirt and white sweater with the big brown "P" on the front.

The heat was mounting now, and the boys on the bench could see the first team sweating. That was the trouble with Kansas weather. It could be up to a hundred in late September and freezing by the middle of October.

Across the field the Wykoff squad had two elevens running through formations. Their green jerseys made them look bigger than real life, and they moved with a lot of snap and precision. At length the officials came strolling from the gym, and the captains were called to midfield for the toss of the coin. The visitors won and chose to receive, while Mike Hoban, the Cowboy defensive captain, picked the west end of the field, with a favoring breeze.

Mary Ann led a long cheer as the two teams took their positions, and Aaron Weil placed the ball for the kickoff. He was a solidly built Jewish boy, quiet and studious, but Tod had seen him crash the line and knew he was all fullback. He also did most of Prairie's kicking.

34

There was a hush, broken by the shrilling of the referee's whistle. Then Weil's foot met the ball, and it sailed toward the Wildcats' goal. A fast little back took it on the five and sprinted upfield twenty yards before he was brought down.

The first play from scrimmage started as a smash at left guard. Big Chris Olsen, the left tackle, charged through, only to be neatly mouse-trapped, and the runner came barreling through till Joe Luke stopped him after a good gain. It was second and two.

Tod could imagine what was being said to Chris in the huddle, and something told him their opponents would try the same play again. Sure enough the ball was passed off to a halfback, who hesitated one count for the trap to take place, so that he could run through left tackle. This time Chris wasn't fooled. He checked his charge and met the ballcarrier head-on, squarely on the line of scrimmage.

With third down and two to go, the big Wildcat quarterback drove over center to pick up all but a foot of the distance. Then, instead of punting on fourth down, he carried the ball again and made it.

That was the way it went for another series of downs and then another. The heavier Wykoff backs kept grinding out short yardage until they were on the Cowboys' twenty-yard line. There the defense stiffened, with the line charging desperately. Suddenly, with third down and five yards to go, Tod saw the quarterback fake to his fullback, then run to his left as if to throw.

"Pass!" yelled Flick Davis, and the linebackers hurried to cover the receivers. But the quarterback kept on running in a wide sweep, with interference ahead of him. It was up to Rudy Ryker now. He tried awkwardly to take out the first blocker and did slow him somewhat, but he himself was knocked down. The other blocker took out Fortunato, and the ballcarrier was still going. He cut inside Flick Davis, the safety man, and Flick's tackle came too late. The Wildcat quarterback was over the goal line.

After the extra point was kicked, the Cowboys were trailing by seven to nothing, and there was gloom on the bench, though the first team appeared undaunted. Andy Willis took the kickoff on the twelve, sprinted past two tacklers, and dodged toward the sideline, where Mike Hoban gave him a key block. The little end made it all the way to midfield before he went down under an avalanche of tacklers.

The fine runback put new spirit into the hometown rooters. They cheered lustily as the Cowboys struggled forward to a first down. Then the attack stalled. The Wykoff coach had put in fresh players, just as big and tough as those who had started. With a third down and six to go, Flick tried a pass to Willis. The blitz was on, and a high-leaping forward tipped the ball as it left the quarterback's hand. It flew right into a Wildcat back's arms, and he had a clear field all the way to the goal line. Fourteen to nothing was the score as the first quarter ended.

Changing sides, Wykoff was able to kick off with the wind, and the ball bounced near the ten-yard line. Luckily the roll took it over the goal before any downfield Wildcat could stop it, and the Cowboys took over on their own twenty. It was encouraging to see the linemen buckle down to work. They pushed those big forwards back on their heels and made holes for Fortunato and Weil to buck through. After crunching out two first downs, each time by inches, Flick called for a trap play. The Wildcat left guard, smarting from being shoved around, charged like an express train and hit nothing. When he picked himself up, bewildered, Joe Luke had plunged through the gap and reached Wykoff territory with a first down.

Dutch Kleinschmidt got off the bench. "Ross," he said, "warm up. Come on—snap to it! You'll go in after the next play."

36

4

Tod's heart was hammering and his knees felt like rubber when he trotted out to the huddle and told Ryker he was to go back to the bench.

"Coach send in a play?" asked Flick.

"Nope. Said it was up to you."

The players' heads were bent over in the circle. "All right," Flick told them. "Let's try twenty-three. Got it, Tod?"

He nodded, and as the huddle broke up, he ran toward the right sideline. "Twenty-three" was a pass to the split end. He waited, listening, as the signals were barked out. At the snap of the ball, he was off and running. One linebacker hurried over, but Tod shot by him, still sprinting. Then he looked over his shoulder and saw the ball arching toward him. His hands went up, and he grabbed it over his head. Just then a tackler crashed into him, and he fell out of bounds, still clutching the pigskin.

As he picked himself up, he heard a shrill yell from the Prairie cheering section. He had made a first down. The ball was placed on the twenty-two.

"OK," panted Flick in the huddle. "They're off balance. This one'll be for you, Andy—down and in."

Tod played at tight end this time. He made a run past the

opposing end and tried to act as if he were the receiver. Over on the other side of the line, he could see Andy Willis darting toward the goal. Then, just as a host of green jerseys swarmed in on him, Flick got rid of the ball in a bullet pass. Andy had played the pattern perfectly and swerved in toward the center of the field. But the ball missed his outstretched fingertips.

"My fault," Flick gasped as they huddled. "They were in on me too quick: Sorry, Andy. How about number six, off tackle, Aaron?"

The fullback nodded, and they lined up again. Tod got

ready to block out the end, and Mike Hoban crouched, preparing to charge. The play went right, and Weil gained a solid five yards.

Now the quarterback called for another plunge, this time to the left. "Want to get in front of the goalposts," he said. "Just in case."

Fortunato carried and slugged out two yards, to the fifteen. It was fourth down.

"How's your toe, Aaron?" Flick asked.

"OK, I guess. But you guys in the line better hold 'em!"

They lined up in tight formation to protect the kicker, and Flick knelt to hold the ball for a placement. The Wildcats charged hard, but Weil's precision kick split the uprights. It was fourteen to three.

That was how the score still stood at half time. In the locker room Kleinschmidt paced up and down while the tired players rested. Tod saw Andy Willis slumped in the darkest corner of the room, his face in his hands, and he moved over beside the end.

"Tired, Andy?" he asked.

Andy shook his head miserably. "Not so tired. Just sick about missin' that pass. We oughta had a touchdown."

"Shucks!" Tod told him. "Nobody could have caught it. Flick couldn't aim because they were blitzing him—that's all. Wait till this next half."

The coach didn't have much to say. "You made a few mistakes," he told them, "but not too many for the first game. You had a couple of bad breaks, too. Maybe the breaks'll even up. All I ask is that you keep on trying. I'm not discouraged, and I don't want you to be."

The hot wind had shifted and was blowing straight across the field when they went out again. Clouds of dust whirled into their faces.

It was Wyoff's turn to kick off, and they encountered a bit of trouble. First the ball fell off the tee. Then it was blown over the sideline, and they had to kick again, this time from the thirty-five after the penalty. As a result the kick was short. Andy Willis took the ball on his own forty and ran like a scalded cat. In an instant he was past his blockers and had to dodge and double to avoid tacklers. But amazingly he made it to the enemy's twenty-five before he was caught.

"Great work, Andy, boy!" his mates told him as they gathered in the huddle. "Come on, Flick—let's go!"

"OK," he told them. "I'm going to scramble. I'll rattle off a flock of signals, an', Link, you hand me the ball on the sixth number. Let's hope they try to blitz. You split out to the right, Ross, an' give me a block. If I'm trapped, I'll pass to you."

They lined up to a steady chorus of "We want a touch-down!" from the hometown fans. At his lonesome spot near the sideline, Tod waited for the snap of the ball, with a tingle in his bones. From the way the defense was dancing around, he knew they meant to rush the passer.

Flick took the ball, dodged back as if looking for a receiver, then sprinted to his right. Mike Hoban took out the end, and Tod hurled himself across the linebacker's knees. By the time he was back on his feet, Flick had darted by and was headed for pay dirt. He made it across the goal line without a hand being laid on him.

They jumped and whooped and pounded one another on the back till Flick steadied them down in the huddle.

"No sense in going for a two-pointer," he said. "We'd still be behind. But let's make mighty sure of that placement!"

Aaron Weil measured his two steps and met the ball squarely. And the score was fourteen to ten.

The Wykoff team came roaring back after the kickoff. One first down after another was made on ground plays, and meanwhile they used up a lot of time. At the start of the last quarter they had advanced to the Prairie fifteen.

40

"Hold that line—hold that line!" chanted the rooters hoarsely. And somehow the weary Cowboys held. With third down and four to go, everyone knew there had to be a pass. Tod tried to remember what he should do on defense. Just hit 'em and knock 'em down, he decided. The Wildcats' left end tried to get by him and was taken out by a clean block. But a halfback had sneaked past, going like the wind. In spite of a mob of Prairie defenders, the quarterback launched his pass, and it was caught for another touchdown.

This time the place-kicker missed his target, and the score stood at twenty to ten.

"Don't get discouraged, gang—there's still time," Flick told them. "Give us another good runback, Andy, an' we'll show 'em!"

The swift little end did his best. He took the ball almost to midfield before he was downed. On the next play Tod went out for a pass, but Flick was snowed under, ten yards back. A line play failed to gain, and a good flare pass to Andy left them short of a first down. They had to kick.

Weil's punt went to the ten, where a fair catch was made. In two ground plays the Wildcats got it out to the fifteen, and again Tod knew a pass was coming. At the snap of the ball, he tore in to rush the passer. Mike Hoban got there ahead of him and leaped high, with both hands above his head. His fingers must have deflected the course of the ball, for suddenly Tod saw it in the air, right in front of him. He grabbed it, juggled it, then caught it again.

Ahead of him there was nothing but dusty earth, and he started to run with all his might. Nothing he had ever done —not even winning the calf roping—gave him the thrill of that moment. He sped over the last white line and banged the ball down in the end zone with the roar of the crowd ringing in his ears.

Weil's boot made the score twenty to seventeen, and the

breathless Cowboys lined up once more to kick off. Time was getting short now, and they needed that ball again.

"Onside kick!" Flick whispered. "Pass the word!"

Tod didn't know exactly what it meant, but he was keyed up, ready for whatever might happen. Weil came up to the ball and kicked it sidewise, only a dozen yards in all. And the Prairie line rushed down in an effort to fall on it.

It seemed their luck had run out, however. A Wykoff tackle got there a split second ahead, and when the pile was untangled, he had it tucked under his body.

"Two minutes to go!" the referee warned, and after the time-out the Wildcat quarter sent his fullback into the middle of the line for three yards. The green-shirts huddled, then came out in leisurely fashion for the next play. With a sinking heart, Tod knew they were running out the clock, and there was nothing he could do about it.

Three more yards were made against a desperate Prairie defense, then two yards, still on the ground. A fourth down was coming up, but the Wildcats had no intention of kicking. They took even more time in the huddle and laughed when the officials penalized them five yards for delay of the game. The time was down to seconds now. The frustrated Cowboys held them for no gain, but before they could take over the ball the final gun sounded.

It was a despondent crowd of players who straggled back to the gym. They showered and started to dress in glum silence. Then Coach Kleinschmidt came in, and to their surprise he was smiling cheerfully.

"Come on," he said, "get rid of those long faces. Whether you think so or not, you all played a great game. I knew Wykoff was one of the toughest teams on our schedule. In fact, I expected a real shellacking, and yet in that second half you played them off their feet! A little bit more luck and you'd have trimmed them. So I'm proud of you, and before this season's over, I think you'll be proud of your-

42

selves. Get some rest this weekend, and we'll talk over our mistakes when you come back Monday."

They all felt a little better when they started home. In the truck Mike turned to Tod with a grin.

"That touchdown you made was a honey," he said. "Sure took 'em by surprise!"

"All I did was grab it an' run," Tod replied. "You're the one who hit the ball over where I could reach it. How about little Andy, though? Boy, how he can scoot!"

"Yep, he's fast all right. Ran the hundred in under ten seconds last spring."

Mike yawned as they neared the Ross ranch. "I'm bushed," he said. "I'd sleep till noon tomorrow if I didn't have to go to Mass. So long, now. See you Monday morning."

Tod found his father at work in the big corral behind the barn. There were still a few calves to be branded.

"Well," Jim Ross growled, "I reckon you got licked."

"That's right, but how'd you know it so quick?"

"A couple of cars full of Wykoff kids went by honkin' their horns an' yellin'. How bad was it?"

"Twenty to seventeen. We almost caught up in the last half."

"Hmm," his father grunted. "Well, go rope me a couple o' dogies while my iron's hot."

No more was said until after supper, when the cattleman had his pipe drawing. "How'd you make out in the game?" he asked. "Did you get to play?"

"Yeah, I got in. Did better'n I thought I would. Made one touchdown on an intercepted pass."

Again there was silence while Jim Ross puffed at his briar. "Who do you play next week?" he inquired at length.

"Logansville, I think. We have to go over there to play on their field."

"Well," said the rancher, "that's not much of a school.

Maybe you can beat 'em. If you do, I'll try an' come to your next game at home."

Tod tried not to show it, but secretly he was pleased. If he could get his father interested in football, perhaps life would be a little easier for him.

*   *   *

"All right, gang," the coach told them in the locker room on Monday. "Let's see if we did anything wrong in that game with Wykoff. What do you say, Mike?"

The big tackle was thoughtful. "I'd say we didn't give Flick enough protection on passes," he commented. "He was rushed too much."

Kleinschmidt nodded. "What about the backfield, Tony? Any criticisms?"

"Well, I guess our timing wasn't too good. I missed the hand-off once or twice. We'd better work on that."

"Good," said the coach. "Now I've got a couple. When you were on defense, they were pushing you back. Sure, I know those forwards were big, but a hard, low charge might have held 'em to fewer yards on the ground. This week you won't be outweighed."

Andy Willis raised his hand. "Reckon I didn't run fast enough on that pass I missed," he said. "I can get out there quicker when I really try."

His remark brought a chorus of denials. "You sure did all right," and "It wasn't your fault, Andy." And Flick had the last word. "You can't catch 'em if I don't throw to you," he said. "We better get some practice on it this week."

"Let's suit up and go out there," Kleinschmidt told them. "No scrimmage—just signal practice and run through some plays. We don't have to get down to hard work until tomorrow. Ross, here's an old football. You and Willis take it and practice some tough pass catches."

Out on the field, Andy pranced and grinned. "Gimme a

44

long one," he called. "Bet you can't throw it over my head!"

As he sprinted away, Tod drew back his arm and arched a forty-yard pass that looked as if it would go far beyond the diminutive end. To his amazement Andy gauged the ball perfectly, reached the right spot, and took it in full flight. His face wore a wide smile as he turned at the goal line and trotted back.

"Now here's one for you," he called. The pass was wobbly but long enough, and it swerved to Tod's left. He moved with it, judging the wild trajectory as best he could. Then his hands reached up, and he caught the ball over his head.

For an hour they kept it up, each trying to put one past the receiver and rarely succeeding. Tod felt that he was learning something with every throw he caught. After a while the coach came over to watch.

"Good going, boys," he said. "We'll see how you do tomorrow, when you have to catch the ball in the middle of a bunch of guys who want to take it away from you."

5

In the corridor on his way to his homeroom next morning, Tod heard a quick step behind him.

"Hi, Tod," said Mary Ann Foster as she came alongside. "I've been hoping I'd see you—just to say what a swell game you played on Saturday."

She paused, somewhat out of breath, and her glance fell. Then she went on quickly. "I know where you live, because I saw the ranch Sunday when we went for a drive out that way. I guess you're a real cowboy, aren't you? Mike said you took a first prize at the Gunstock Rodeo!"

"Yep," said Tod, flushing, "that's so. The way you led the cheering at the game sort of helped us play better. Too bad we couldn't have won."

They had reached the door by then, and other students were pushing past them. "I've got to go in," Tod told her hurriedly. "But I hope I'll get a chance to talk to you again. So long, now!"

Tod had never paid much attention to girls. He didn't dance or go to parties, outside of an occasional barbecue or sociable. And life on the ranch gave him everything he wanted. There was riding and roping, hunting jackrabbits, fishing and swimming in Smoky Hill River. After his mother

46

died when he was four, the only woman he really knew was plain, middle-aged Mrs. McDonald, who did their cooking and cleaning. In such movies as he had seen, there were beautiful girls, of course, but they weren't real to him. Mary Ann was a new experience.

In history class he stole a long look at her, where she sat a row ahead of him on his right. He noticed with some surprise that her long blond hair shone like silk, that there was a dusting of freckles across her nose, and that under her sweater her slender body was curved in the right places. All this disturbed him in a strange, pleasant way.

Perhaps it was fortunate that at that moment Miss Brown, the history teacher, called his name.

"Tod Ross," she said, "can you tell us who wrote the final draft of the Declaration of Independence?"

He gulped and tried to gather his wits. "I think—it was Benjamin Franklin—maybe?" he stammered.

Several hands went up, and Miss Brown pointed to Mary Ann.

"It was Thomas Jefferson," she answered. "But I'm sure Ben Franklin did help with some of the ideas."

She looked back fleetingly at Tod, and the apology he saw in her brown eyes made him feel better. He waited after the period was over, but Mary Ann was talking to Miss Brown, so he left for his next class.

At three that afternoon he dressed for football practice, and for the next hour and a half he was too busy to think about girls. There was a good, hard scrimmage to sharpen up the line play. Afterward Coach Kleinschmidt told the scrub team to break up Flick's passing attack if they could.

The method they used was to leave only four men on the line and concentrate the seven others in the backfield to cover receivers. Tod found himself surrounded by two or three eager defenders every time he started downfield after a pass. Once he made a leaping catch and got away for a long gain, but more often the ball was batted down or nearly intercepted.

The same tactics were being used on Andy Willis at left end, so Flick decided to cross them up. He had Tod and Andy run forward as usual, then passed neatly over center to Joe Luke. It was an easy first down, and the varsity got another a moment later with a flare pass to Tony Fortunato.

"Good!" said the coach. "That's using your head, Flick! Of course, you'll never run into that kind of pass defense, but if they do pull back to cover, remember a good end sweep'll make yardage, too."

The week seemed to go fast. Every night Tod changed into his work clothes and hurried out to help with the corn harvest. Jim Ross believed in growing his stock feed right on the place, and he had over forty acres in corn. Now that the kernels had ripened and hardened, the ears had to be picked, and Tod was good at it. He and another man, walking on either side of the truck, jerked the corn from the stalks, ripped off the husks, and tossed the yellow ears up against the "bang-board."

Even with cotton gloves on, the pickers' hands took a beating, and Tod's back also was tired by the time he fell into bed.

There was no scrimmage on Friday, so Mike drove him home early. The clouds were gray and threatening, and a sharp wind blew from the north when Tod rode out to the cornfield.

"Come on!" his father yelled. "Got to finish tonight if we can. There's rain comin'."

Five o'clock passed and six o'clock, but nobody thought of supper. By the head lamps of the truck and a makeshift floodlight, mounted above the center bang-board, the tired pickers worked on till after ten that night. Then, as the last load was hustled toward the barn, spits of cold, hard-driven rain began to pelt them.

"Don't look like much of a day for football tomorrow," Jim Ross observed grumpily. "Reckon you'll wish you was snug at home."

"They don't call off a game when it rains," Tod replied. "An' we wouldn't if we could. This time we aim to win one. Good night, Pa. I've got to get some sleep."

Tod was ravenous the next morning. Looking out at the steady rain, he put away oatmeal, sausages, and pancakes, and felt better fortified. At eleven o'clock Mike Hoban honked his horn from the road, and Tod ran out to join him.

"Goin' to have to run in the mud today," Mike remarked cheerfully. "Hope you turn out to be a mudder, Tod."

"Guess I won't know till I try," Tod chuckled. "Anyhow, it'll be just as slippery for the other guys."

The boys stopped at "Joe's Giant Hamburgers" for a light lunch, then drove on to school. There was a bus waiting there to take the squad to Logansville, a dozen miles to the south. The football manager had already packed their gear aboard.

As he climbed in out of the rain, Tod saw the little Prairie High band and the girl cheerleaders carrying their dripping instruments and their megaphones toward a second bus. Mary Ann, in a green raincoat, was among them, but she didn't look his way, and he didn't want to call to her. A moment later the two vehicles were in motion.

By the time they reached Logansville, the rain had subsided to a chill drizzle. The football manager hurried to the gymnasium and came back with a downcast look.

"There's no locker room for visiting teams," he announced. "We'll have to dress in the bus."

There was general grumbling at this news, but Mike Hoban merely grinned. "Guess we just have to beat 'em that much worse," he said, "an' teach 'em some politeness."

"It's all right, boys," the coach told them. "They don't spend money on schools here, and the gym isn't much better than a barn, anyhow. You're lucky to have a warm bus. Come on, now. I want everybody on the field in half an hour."

The Logansville Lions at least had new uniforms of red and gold, and Tod thought they looked pretty smart as they warmed up, then got ready to receive Prairie's kickoff. Grimly he wondered how they would appear after a few tackles in the mud. Then he was running down under the kick. It was a low, erratic one that bounced crazily. A Lion back got his hands on it for a second before it squirted out of his grasp—a free ball! Tod picked up the slippery oval and clutched it in both arms as he ran. Then, almost before he knew it, he had scored a touchdown.

Wet but exuberant, the Cowboys lined up in front of the goalposts, and Aaron Weil sent the ball over the bar. Then Prairie kicked off again. Logansville held onto the ball this time, but their attack bogged down on the thirty, and they had to punt. Andy Willis also muffed the ball in trying to make a fair catch, but he fell on it after dropping it.

Back on his own fifteen, Flick called for an off-tackle plunge, and the line opened a hole that let Joe Luke slither through. Then Fortunato hit the other side for enough yardage to give them a first down.

"Think you could hang onto a pass?" the quarterback asked Tod. "They figure we don't dare throw in this rain, an' they've got the defense pulled in."

"I can try," Tod answered.

"OK, line up at tight end, but go for the sideline. Then on the next play don't come into the huddle—just stay out there all alone. Maybe they won't see you."

Tod made his run to the right while the play was being stopped in the middle of the line. A yard from the side stripe he stood motionless and watched his teammates huddle. Every second he expected somebody to notice him and yell a warning, but none did. Then the teams lined up, and at the snap he was off, sprinting downfield but watching over his shoulder. Flick got off a long floater that nestled lightly into his hands, and to his amazement the nearest defender was a good ten yards away. All he had to do was run in a straight line to the goal, some sixty yards away. He made it, winded but happy, and a moment later the score was fourteen to nothing, with less than five minutes gone.

Somewhat dazed by all this, the Lions got ready to receive again. There was mud on their beautiful gold pants

and red jerseys, but as soon as they got the ball, they showed they were still in the game. A well-executed end sweep came toward Tod's position, and when his feet slipped, he missed taking out the blocker. By the time Flick came up from safety to tackle the ballcarrier, the play had gone for twenty yards.

Tod was angry with himself. He picked chunks of mud out of his cleats and waited for another chance. It came right away, for the Lions must have figured they had found a weak spot. Once more the left halfback had the ball and was coming around Tod's end with two blockers in front of him.

Tod set his teeth and charged, with Joe Luke close behind him. In a split second he saw that the two men running interference were close together, and he timed his stride and dove sidewise. His body and outstretched legs cut them both down, so that Luke could nail the ballcarrier right at the line of scrimmage.

Logansville's attack slowed down short of the fifty-yard line, and they were forced to punt. After that it was all Prairie through the rest of the half. Weil plunged over for one touchdown, and Andy Willis added another. The score was twenty-seven to nothing when the muddy but happy Cowboys returned to their bus at half time.

"Scrape off your shoes," Dutch told them. "Then get some rest. I'm not going to give you any lecture because you did most things right. My only warning is, don't get overconfident and let down. They'll be sore and out for blood this half."

It didn't take long to find out how right he was. Prairie received the kickoff and hit a stone wall on the first two line plays. When Flick dropped back to pass, three men poured through and knocked him flat for a twelve-yard loss. And finally Weil was rushed so hard on his first punt that the wobbly ball fell short of the midfield stripe. Then, almost before the bewildered Cowboys could line up, a hard-driving back broke through for a first down.

"Hey, guys—what's happened to you?" Flick asked in the defensive huddle. "Get in there and fight!"

They held better on the next series of downs, but a pass into the flat made the needed yardage. It was the first pass the Lions had tried, and its success gave them heart. After failing to gain past the twenty by rushing, their quarterback drifted sidewise and lobbed a pass over Tony Fortunato's head. An end had sprinted along the sideline and was there to catch it. Flick couldn't quite reach him, and he went over for a touchdown.

With the score twenty-seven to seven, Flick called a time-out and went over for a word with the coach. When he returned, he looked grave but resolute.

"They've got momentum now," he told the players, "and we'll have to do something to break it up. Dutch thinks they may try an onside kick, so you guys in the line watch for it."

Tod could see the ball being teed up at an angle, and he edged in closer to Mike Hoban. Then the whistle blew, and the kicker was trotting forward. The ball squirted sidewise and bounced straight into Tod's waiting hands. Its wet surface was like the hide of a greased pig, but he got a firm grip as he ran.

"Go, boy!" yelled Mike, blocking out a pursuer, and Tod went. His touchdown, coming just when the Lions were getting started, seemed to shatter their morale, and they never recovered the initiative again.

Even though Kleinschmidt put in some of his second-stringers, by the time the game ended, the score had climbed to forty-one to seven. And while the Logansville players were glum, their local backers were furious. Mud balls began to fly. It took all Dutch's steadying influence to get his boys into the bus without a general fight.

Those who had come on the other bus weren't so fortunate. Tod was just climbing aboard when he saw a little freshman trumpet player being manhandled by two bigger boys, and he dashed back to do something about it. But the fracas was all over before he got there. He saw Mary Ann Foster tear in like an avenging angel, whirling her big megaphone. She knocked one of the bullies down and chased the other off.

"Hi, Tod!" she called gaily. "Thanks for coming, but I reckon they've had enough. Come on, Johnny. Pick up your horn case and get in the bus."

The rain stopped about the time they got moving, and pale sunshine, coming through the windows, soothed their tempers. In a moment someone started a song. Before they reached Prairie, the disagreeable aftermath of their victory had been forgotten.

"Golly!" said Tod as he stripped off his mud-caked jersey in the locker room. "Do you think these things'll ever come clean again?"

"Don't worry," Mike told him. "The girls have still got washers an' dryers down in the Home Ec. Department. An' after those three touchdowns you scored, they'll prob'ly send your suit back smellin' of perfume!"

The hot shower and dry clothes made Tod feel better. When he got home, he found his father had come in from work and was waiting for him.

"Well," he asked gruffly, "how bad was it this time?"

Tod laughed. "Not too bad," he replied. "We won, forty-one to seven."

"What! Six touchdowns? They couldn't have been much good. Did you get to play?"

"Yep. The whole game."

"An' did you help any?"

"I reckon so," Tod told him with a straight face. "I scored three o' the touchdowns."

54

There was a moment's silence while Jim Ross tried to digest this news. If he was impressed, he did his best not to show it. But Tod thought he saw a gleam of pride in his eyes.

"Well," his father said at length, "maybe now that the worst o' the fall work's over, I can find time to get to a game. Who do you play next week?"

"The Juliana Jaybirds," Tod told him. "Ought to be a pretty good game, an' we'll be playing at home. I sure hope you can be there."

6

Early the next morning, Tod's father drove into town for the Sunday paper—something he rarely did. While he still pretended to be scornful of football, Tod noticed that he was reading the sports section with some care. At length he flung the paper down with a snort.

"Back there in Wichita," he commented, "they don't seem to know anybody plays football except the pros, an' colleges, an' their own high schools. Last time I'll waste money on this sheet!"

Tod picked up the paper and finally found a half-inch item at the bottom of the fourth sports page. "Cowboys Take Lions" was the tiny headline, and it was followed by the bare announcement that Prairie had beaten Logansville. Even then the score was wrong. A careless typesetter had given it as "14-7," reversing the first two figures.

"Oh, well," Tod thought with a grin, "maybe by the end of the season they'll think we're more important."

On Monday the squad was given a breather, taking a few laps around the field, then listening to the coach as he gave them an account of what they might expect from the Juliana Jaybirds.

"They're pretty big," he said, "but they don't have much

overall speed. One of their backs is about as fast as Andy, here, but he's the only one. From what I know of their coach, he won't be likely to use any very tricky plays. His boys know their fundamentals, though. You'll find they block well and tackle hard. Even if we get a dry field, we ought to have our hands full. How's everybody feel? Any injuries?"

Outside of a couple who complained of pulled muscles, the first eleven all seemed to be in good shape.

"All right," Dutch said, "go home and rest up for some hard work tomorrow. If you can stay a minute, Tod, I'd like a word with you and Flick."

Tod waited, wondering if he had done something wrong in the Logansville game.

"I've been wondering about that lonesome end play," Dutch began. "Of course, it worked beautifully, but they weren't looking for it. Suppose we use it oftener, Flick—think it would go?"

The quarterback considered. "Sure," he said at length. "Tod's a first-class pass-catcher, an' even if the other side saw him out there on the wing, about all they could do would be to send one man over to cover him. That might open the defense up a bit. Of course, not being in the huddle, Tod won't know the play, but maybe I can call audible signals."

"What do you think, Tod?" asked the coach.

"Sure. I kind of like it out there by myself," Tod said with a grin. "We don't have to do it all the time. Just once in a while."

"Right! You'd always be a threat, whether the pass is to you or not," said Dutch. "The way you handle a wet ball, maybe we ought to pray for rain every Saturday!"

All the rest of that week he worked them hard. Flick figured out a system for letting Tod, the split end, know when a pass was coming his way. They agreed that any time Flick called a number in the nineties as the fourth in a series, that would be Tod's signal to get downfield for a pass.

"If they get on to it," the quarterback explained, "I can change the play to something else."

In practice Tod spent a lot of time out on the wing, and even though the scrub team knew what to expect, the play worked against them twice in a row. The third time was different.

As he loped along the sideline, giving Flick time to throw, he heard a sudden pounding of feet behind him. Looking back, he found a big figure in pursuit and saw Rudy Ryker's

58

earnest face, contorted with effort. He also saw the ball floating toward him and spun to his left, preparing to catch it. Rudy turned with him, stretched his tall body upward, and batted the pigskin away.

Tod wasn't angry. "Good boy, Rudy!" he said with a chuckle. "You played that one just right!"

After practice he took time to speak to the coach. "Old Rudy did a nice job on me when he blocked that pass," he said. "I guess he feels pretty low about being dropped off the first team, an' I wondered—couldn't you send him in at end when we're on defense?"

Dutch looked thoughtful. "We need you, too," he said. "But I could shift you back to a corner post an' give Tony or Aaron a rest. We can try it in practice."

"Thanks," Tod said. "I figure Rudy ought to have a chance for his letter, the way he works."

"We'll see," Kleinschmidt answered.

*　*　*

"Hi, Tod," Mary Ann greeted him next day as they were going into history class. "You know all about calves, don't you?"

He grinned. "Well, I've seen a few of 'em," he said. "Why?"

"I've got one I'm raising," she told him. "A little Guernsey heifer. She's my 4-H project. And I wondered if you couldn't come over to our house and see her. You can probably give me some good advice. You know where we live? It's only a mile west of town."

They were inside now, taking their seats. "OK," Tod whispered. "Tonight, after supper."

He got most of his school assignments done in homeroom. Then came football practice, and when it was over, he rode home as usual with Mike. On the way he watched for the Foster place and saw the name on the mailbox. It wasn't a real farm, but the big house stood in a handsome tract of eight or ten acres, and there was a barn at the rear.

"Tryin' to catch a glimpse of your girl?" Mike asked teasingly.

"Not really," Tod replied. "Just wondered where she lived."

"Nice place," Mike commented. "Wade Foster owns the tractor agency in town, so I reckon he's well heeled."

As soon as supper was over, Tod put on a clean shirt and combed his hair.

"Got to go out for a bit," he told his father. "I'll be home 'fore long."

He saddled the buckskin and rode eastward along the soft shoulder of the highway. He entered the driveway of the Foster home and tied his pony to the porch rail. At his knock, a big bald-headed man in shirt sleeves came to the door.

"Oh," he said, "you must be the youngster Mary Ann said would be here. Come in. What's your name—Ross?"

"Yes, sir, I'm Jim Ross's son."

He sat on the edge of a chair, his big hands twisting his Stetson. It was the first time he had ever called at a girl's home.

"Hi, Tod!" Mary Ann called from the stairs. "Have you met my father? Dad, this is Tod Ross, in my class at school. He's come over to look at Buttercup."

Mr. Foster smiled. "Yes, dear, we've met," he said. "And I hope he approves of the calf."

Awkwardly Tod had risen, and now he followed the girl out to the barn. The wide barn door stood open, and she pressed a light switch as they went in.

"She's over here," Mary Ann told him. "In the box stall. I give her lots of milk, and she's learned to eat cracked corn, too."

The calf looked very small to Tod, used to beef cattle.

60

She was a golden tan in color, with white patches, and her big brown eyes looked at them, half eagerly, half in fear.

"She's mighty pretty," he commented. "But awful little, isn't she?"

Mary Ann sniffed and gave her blond hair a toss. "Buttercup's nearly six months old," she said. "Trouble is, you don't know a fine Guernsey heifer when you see one. She's a purebred, and her mother was a champion!"

"You're right about my not knowing much." Tod laughed. "But I did say she was pretty—most as pretty as an antelope. You aim to show her at the 4-H Fair?"

"Yes, indeed, and she'll take a blue ribbon, I bet." Mary Ann was in the stall now, letting the calf nuzzle her hand. "You'll win, won't you, beautiful?" she crooned. "Got to leave you now, but sleep well!"

She shut the gate of the stall and took Tod's arm. "I forgive you for not appreciating my little Buttercup," she said. "Come on in the house, now. I made some lemonade and cookies."

It had been a hot day for October, though Tod knew the night would be chilly later. The lemonade tasted good, and Mary Ann did her best to entertain him. She even turned on the record player and tried to teach him one of the new dance gyrations, much to her parents' amusement.

"OK," Tod panted after a while. "It's been fun, but I have to get to bed early. Big practice tomorrow."

"That's right, daughter," Wade Foster put in. "You want him to make some more touchdowns against those Jaybirds, so you'd better let him go."

Tod rode home with mixed emotions. He felt he had cut a pretty poor figure attempting to dance, and he was sorry he hadn't shown more enthusiasm for the Guernsey calf. On the other hand, he couldn't help being pleased that such a pretty girl seemed to like his company. Most of the way home, he whistled the old melody of "Aura Lee" and managed to get up to bed without having to answer any questions from his father.

Mike Hoban had a mischievous twinkle in his eye when Tod swung aboard the truck the next morning.

"Well, how'd they treat you at Fosters'," he asked casually.

"Who said anything about the Fosters?" Tod replied. "Just because I looked at the house doesn't mean I went calling."

"That right? Well, somebody must ha' borrowed your pony, then. I had an errand to do in town last night, an' durned if your ol' buckskin wasn't tied in front!"

Tod grinned. "OK," he said. "I was there to take a look at Mary Ann's little heifer calf. But you'd better not spread the news around school if you want us to stay friends."

"Trust me, kid," the big tackle answered. "I won't breathe a word."

Almost before they knew it, the week was ending and the Juliana game was upon them. The weather was cold but fair, and the stands were filling up with loyal Prairie rooters when the visitors' cars and buses began to arrive.

Tod, getting into his uniform in the locker room, wondered whether his father would come to the game. When he had left home at noon, the issue was still in doubt.

"Got to ride fence today," Jim Ross had said at breakfast. "If I'm through in time, I might come to town an' see part of it."

Dutch Kleinschmidt entered and looked around at the squad. "Hustle it up, boys," he said. "I want you out on the field. What I'd like to see is a good, snappy signal drill before game time."

They put on their shoes, picked up their helmets, and went clumping out, while a long yell of encouragement came from the cheering section. In a moment the first and second teams had lined up and were running through simple patterns, trying merely for precision and quick starts.

Across the field the Jaybirds, resplendent in dark blue and light blue uniforms, were galloping about, shoving each other and turning somersaults to loosen up. Tod stole a look at them and decided they were even bigger than the Wykoff team that had beaten them in their first game.

"What do those guys weigh?" Joe Luke mumbled in the lineup.

"Don't let 'em scare you," Flick told him. "Dutch says they're too heavy to be fast."

Tod kept his own counsel. With a line like that, he figured they could score on the ground, so it was up to Prairie to score more points with speed, deception, and good passing.

A short time later the referee called the captains out to toss a coin. Juliana won and chose to receive. There was little wind, so Flick chose the end of the field with the sun behind them. And after the Cowboy band had played the National Anthem, the team lined up to kick.

"Keep your eye on that guy Casey," Flick ordered. "He's the speed merchant."

Casey looked tall and slender as he waited on his ten-yard line to take the kick. Aaron Weil got plenty of power into it, and the ball sailed high and long. Tod was down the field fast. He easily dodged a pair of bulky blockers and was about to tackle Casey when the elusive back spun away and started for the far sideline. Somehow he avoided Andy Willis and kept on going. By the time Joe Luke finally tackled him, he had crossed the thirty-five-yard line.

"We were lucky," Flick told them in the defensive huddle. "He ran one back for a touchdown last week."

On the first play from scrimmage, the Jaybirds bulldozed a hole in the Prairie line, and their bulky fullback plunged through for eight yards.

"Get under 'em!" Mike Hoban urged. "Hit 'em low an' hard!"

The line charged better on the next play and allowed an advance of only two yards. But that was enough for a first down. So it went for the next few minutes—the Jays rushing, the Cowboys giving up ground grudgingly. The blue-clad team was on the nine now, first down and goal to go.

"Hold that line! Hold that line!" screamed the hometown students, while rooters across the field yelled, "We want a touchdown!"

As the groggy Cowboys went into their defensive huddle, Rudy Ryker came running on the field. "Coach sent me in to let you take a breather," he told Tod.

"Good!" Tod panted. "Give 'em what for, Rudy!"

Then, from the sideline, he watched the visitors line up. They hadn't tried a single pass, so the Prairie defense was massed with seven men on the line. At the snap, the big fullback lunged forward, heading for an expected gap between Hoban and Ryker. There was no hole there. Shoulder to shoulder, the right tackle and end stonewalled the play to a halt, and bedlam broke loose in the stands.

"Yea, Rudy!" yelled Tod, though nobody heard him above the din.

Gallantly the Prairie line held its ground, but the ball inched forward. On fourth down, the Jaybirds had only a yard to go. The quarterback took the snap and literally dove over the locked linemen for a touchdown.

The placement for the extra point went wide. and the score was six to nothing when the Cowboys took their places to receive the kickoff. Tod was back in again now, rested enough so that he felt he could lick his weight in saber-toothed tigers.

The kick was taken by Andy. He cut diagonally across the field, picked up a solid block from Mike Hoban, and was over the fifty before they could stop him.

64

Tod was on his way back to the huddle when he caught a sign from Flick Davis. He stopped and sauntered slowly toward the sideline. Just inside it he stood still, trying to look like a spectator. Then Flick was calling his signals.

"Twenty-two—sixteen—seven—ninety-three!" he barked, and as the ball was snapped, Tod sped toward the enemy goal.

7

The pass was one of the long, easy floaters that Flick threw so well. Tod was beyond the corner back, almost even with the safety man, when he saw the pass coming. But the safety man was none other than the great Casey. He cut over so fast that he and Tod went up for the football together, and his reaching fingers tipped it to the right. Tod made a desperate lunge, stretched out his right hand, and caught the falling ball before it hit the ground. Then he was slammed down, rolling as he fell. But his strong fingers still held their grip on the pigskin, and he held it high for the officials to see.

The referee had already signaled an incompleted pass. Now, running nearer, he stared at Tod and the ball and changed his mind. He planted a foot at the spot where Tod had hit the turf, and it was inside the five-yard line!

Tod stood up dizzily, his ears throbbing to the yells of the delighted hometowners. Then he found himself in the huddle, with Mike's arm around his shoulders, and Flick was talking urgently. Still too dazed to know what the play would be, Tod lined up beside Mike in a tight end position. The snap came quickly, on the second count, and he saw Andy Willis, out to the left, sprint toward the sideline.

Three big defense men crashed through the line, but Flick sidestepped coolly, took aim, and pitched a bullet, low and hard, just ahead of the swiftly moving end. Andy whirled, snuggled the ball into his middle, and fell forward over the goal line. The score was tied, and when Aaron Weil kicked the extra point, Prairie went ahead, seven to six.

"Yea, Cowboys!" howled the cheering section, with Mary Ann prancing and waving her megaphone on the sideline.

Tod had caught his breath now and felt ready for anything. On the kickoff he was downfield almost as soon as the ball. He saw Casey make the catch and hesitate, looking for blockers, and he saw Andy Willis roaring in from the left. They caught the speedy back from two sides at the same instant, and at the impact of their charge the ball flew out of his arms.

Andy had his head and shoulder buried in Casey's middle, but Tod caught a glimpse of the bouncing pigskin. He rushed after it, picked it off the ground, and ran on without breaking stride. Before any Jaybird could lay a hand on him, he was over for another touchdown.

Everything had taken place so fast that the crowd didn't realize what had happened. For a couple of seconds there was hardly a sound. Then the roar was deafening. Before it died down, another good placement made the score fourteen to six.

In the second quarter, Juliana once more made its plodding march toward Prairie's goal line. Five yards—two—three—and a bare first down. It used up a lot of time, but it was gradually wearing down the Cowboys' stamina, for the men in the line took a brutal pounding. With less than a minute left in the half, the Jaybirds were down to the five-yard line, with second down and goal to go.

There they took time out. Dutch sent in Rudy Ryker to put some bulk in the line and moved Tod back to Fortunato's linebacker spot. The Italian boy was staggering with weariness as he went off the field.

"What do you want me to do, Flick?" Rudy asked eagerly.

"Just knock over anybody that comes around your side," the quarterback told him. "Tod, you watch the play, an' if you see a hole start to open, plug it up."

The two teams lined up again, and Tod sensed something different in the way the Juliana backs were crouching. Could it be a pass? As the ball was snapped, he saw the quarter fake a hand-off to the fullback, then lateral it off to Casey, who was running his way. An end sweep!

"Rudy!" he yelled, but the big fellow had already plunged ahead dutifully to block the opposing tackle. And here came the fast halfback, the ball tucked under his arm. Tod guessed at the distance and left his feet in a diving tackle. It didn't stop Casey, but in trying to avoid Tod, he stepped out of bounds within a yard of the goal.

Tod knew the seconds were ticking off. Hastily the Juliana team started to line up. Then their captain hailed the referee to ask for a time-out, but before he could make himself heard, the gun sounded and the first half was over. While the Jaybird rooters howled their protests, the Prairie cheerleaders led a snake dance onto the field.

"Well, gang," said Coach Kleinschmidt, back in the locker room, "I don't need to tell you we had some luck in that first half. Maybe we've used up all our luck for today. But you played well against a heavier team. All I can say is, even if they score some more points, I'm betting on you to match 'em. I think you sort of shook up that star back of theirs. He acted a little gun-shy when you went for him on that last play, Tod."

"I don't wonder." Andy laughed. "When Tod an' me both hit him that time, we darn' near bust him in two!"

They rested as much as they could before trooping out

68

for the second half. Tod looked hard at the stands, hoping to find his father, but there were too many people milling about. "Maybe he couldn't make it," he told himself with a let-down feeling.

It was the Cowboys' turn to receive the kickoff. "Gimme some blockin'," Andy begged as he left them to drop back to the ten-yard line, and they all resolved they would.

The kick was high but not too long. Watching it, Tod picked out an onrushing tackler and put him out of the play. Then, as he looked around for another victim, he saw Andy dodging across the field, evading one foe after another. He got behind Mike Hoban, and the husky tackle took out the nearest Jaybird. Then Andy put on a burst of speed, coming upfield, close to the sideline. There was only one opponent with a chance to stop him now—the safety man—and it was toward him that Tod charged. He saw Casey hesitate, change direction, and try to run around him to the left. Then there was no need to block him, for Andy had sprinted past!

The touchdown and the point after gave Prairie a solid lead of twenty-one to six.

After that the Jaybirds got the ball and started another series of lumbering ground plays that made one first down after another. It wasn't easy, however, and when they were past midfield, they tried some passes in desperation. Only one out of four succeeded, so they settled down once again to line bucks. Finally they rammed one over. This time the kick was through the uprights. Score: Juliana, thirteen; Prairie, twenty-one.

Taking the kickoff, the Cowboys started on their twenty-five and made one easy first down on a pass to Tod. For two plays they hit the big Jaybird line without success. Then Flick called for another pass.

"They'll be expecting this," he said. "You, Andy and Tod, get downfield and act like receivers. Draw off all the defensive men you can. Joe Luke, I want you to get through into the flat, an' I'll pitch it to you there. And you guys in the line, hold 'em long enough to give me time."

The play almost failed, for the Juliana tackles came through fast to smear the passer. But just as he was hit, Flick got off a high, wild one that Luke had to leap upward to catch. He made the first down, but with only inches to spare.

Passes came harder now, for the Jaybirds were red-dogging on every play. Twice Flick was snowed under for lost yardage. At last, near the fifty-yard line, they were forced to punt. And once more the Juliana juggernaut started to roll.

In spite of all their efforts, the tired Prairie linemen were unable to stem the steady advance. It was halfway through the last quarter when the Jaybirds made their third touchdown and pulled up within a point of Prairie on the scoreboard—twenty to twenty-one. The cheerleaders still whooped it up valiantly, but there was less confidence in the stands.

"What we've got to have right now," Flick told the players in the huddle, "is another touchdown. This game is one we've got to win!"

They spread out to receive the kickoff, and it was a good one. Andy caught it on his own five and ran it out to the twenty-three before he was tackled. From that point the Cowboys ground out a first down to the thirty-five. A pass to Andy was overthrown, and another, intended for Tod, was batted down at the scrimmage line.

Third down now and still ten yards to go. "They're sure we'll pass this time," said Flick in the huddle. "If you're all game, I'm going to line up in shotgun formation and cross them up with a quick kick. We did it in practice—remember? Everybody get down there fast!"

They took their places with three backs spread behind

the line and both ends split. To their opponents the formation meant only one thing—a pass, with five eligible receivers. Flick, ten yards back of the center, barked his signals, caught the ball, and hesitated as if looking for an open pass target. The blue-shirts came galloping through, but with perfect timing he kicked the ball, low and hard.

It flew to the right, just over Tod's head, and he saw a confused pass-defender hurry back after it. The ball struck the ground, bouncing crazily, and when the back grabbed at it, he couldn't hold on. Tod put on speed. It was a free ball now, and he reached it just ahead of the safety man.

He went for it the way he would for a roped calf—with big, sure hands spread—and gripped it to his stomach as he fell. Casey landed on top of him, knocking his wind out, but he kept his hold.

When the referee came and took the ball, Tod lay there gasping. It required a time-out for him to get his wind back and stagger to his feet, but when he looked at the linesmen's sticks, he found that the ball was on the Juliana fifteen-yard line.

His friends gathered about him. "Attaboy, Tod! Great work, Tod!" they told him. And Flick put an arm around his shoulders.

"Here's the guy who made the quick kick work," he said. "Now, what'll we do about it? Tell you what I suggest—a quick flare pass out to Andy Willis. OK?"

The play started well, but the defense moved fast to that side, and Andy gained only half a dozen yards. On the next one, Flick called for the same formation, but this time with a variation. Andy took the lateral, waited till the defending backs had shifted to his side of the field, then cut back to the right like a streak of light. Mike gave him a good block, and he swivel-hipped past the end. The only other man in his way was Casey, and Tod joyfully laid the safety man flat. Andy scampered on over the goal line. Once more Aaron Weil added the extra point that made the score twenty-eight to twenty.

The final minutes of that game were a nightmare of bone-crushing ground attack, met by gritty defense. Fiercely the Jaybirds struggled for first downs, but they had to make them by sheer weight. Tired as they were, the Cowboys fought for every inch. And when the final gun sounded, Juliana was still short of the goal line.

As they limped off the field, the Prairie varsity had to run a gauntlet of hugs from the girl cheerleaders. Tod found himself embraced by Mary Ann Foster, and he entered the locker room as red as a beet.

"What's the matter, boy?" Mike Hoban laughed. "Don't you like it? I'd say you rated that one! Whoopee!"

Then, as Tod sat down to pull off his dripping jersey, he saw a big, square-shouldered figure in front of him.

"How you feel, son?" his father asked huskily.

"Gee, Pa! You did get here! I feel great—how else?"

"OK," said Jim Ross, obviously relieved. "I got a bit worried when you were lyin' there on the ground. Say—

72

I'm glad I came! You boys sure played your heads off. I'd like to meet the rest."

"Sure, Pa. Here, gang, this is Jim Ross, my father." And he introduced them, one by one. "This is our coach, Dutch Kleinschmidt," he added. "I reckon he's happy, too."

The two men shook hands. "Yep," said Dutch. "Happy and proud. These youngsters don't know the word 'quit.' And this boy of yours might turn out to be a pretty fair country football player!"

Tod's father was waiting for him in the car after he showered and dressed.

"How'd you like the game, Pa?" Tod asked as he got in.

"Me? I liked it fine, of course. I got a little fidgety when they scored that last touchdown, but you boys came back strong. Who's that Negro kid? He sure can run."

"That's Andy Willis," Tod replied. "Isn't he something?"

"You're somethin' yourself. I reckon it wasn't such a bad idea for you to go out for football."

They rode in silence for a while. "Let's see," said Jim Ross at length. "You've lost one game an' won two. How many games do you play in all?"

"Eight," Tod told him. "Five more to go."

"Think you can win 'em all?"

"Heck!" said Tod with a chuckle. "That's sort of a big order. But we'll sure try. Some folks said Juliana was the toughest team on the schedule. They were the biggest, all right, but all they knew how to play was straight power football. We'll probably run up against some trickier teams. The Hewlett Owls, for instance. I hear they won today, an' that makes three straight. We play 'em next week on their home grounds. Think you'd be able to get there, Pa?"

"I might," said his father, and left it at that.

8

"This Hewlett team," Coach Kleinschmidt told his squad, "is good. They've won three games, so they're riding high. But I think we can take 'em, once we've learned to handle their plays. They're the only outfit on our schedule that uses a single wing formation. I'm going to try to teach it to the scrubs, so you can practice against it. Now take a look at the blackboard and see how it works."

"The main difference is that the quarterback doesn't stand over the center to take the snap. He's generally in the tailback spot, and the ball is snapped directly to any one of the backfield men. The advantage of that is fast starts for an end run or an off-tackle play. Sometimes they pull a guard out to lead the interference, so they get extra blockers moving ahead of the ballcarrier. Everybody understand?"

"Sure," said Flick Davis. "But there must be something wrong with the single wing or everybody'd be using it."

"It has a few drawbacks—that's true," the coach answered. "They have to have a really good center, or some of his passes'll be muffed. And it's probably easier for the defense to spot where the ball is coming. On the other hand, you won't have as good a chance to blitz the passer. He's already back five yards or more. What we'll do this week is concentrate on defense. I think our offense'll do all right if we have one or two new plays."

The second team worked hard on learning to handle the single wing, but when several of the center's passes went astray, Dutch moved the first-string center, Link Carey, over to the scrubs. For a day or two the varsity had trouble stopping the off-tackle drives. Then Tod and Mike worked out a way to take out that formidable interference, and Andy and Chris Olsen adopted the same plan on their end of the line.

At home, Tod had little time to talk football with his father. After he had done the chores and gotten his homework out of the way, he was usually too tired to keep his eyes open. On Wednesday night he was just ready to go to bed when the telephone rang. He heard his father answer it, then call him.

"It's for you, Tod. Some gal wants to talk to you."

"Who is it?" he whispered with a scowl as he went into the other room. But Jim Ross only shrugged.

"Hi, Tod!" said a lilting voice at the other end of the line. "It's Mary Ann—in case you hadn't guessed. Haven't got a date for this Saturday night, have you? Good! Then you're invited to the Methodist Church supper. I know— I'll be late getting home from the game, too—but they'll be serving up till eight o'clock, so that ought to give us time. And I know it'll be good—I'm cooking some things myself!"

"Gee, I dunno, Mary Ann," he stammered. "I reckon I'll be so bushed, I wouldn't be very good company. An' I'd have to come all the way home first to get on my Sunday clothes."

"Nonsense!" She laughed. "You'll be perfectly all right in your jeans and boots. Please, Tod?"

"Well, thanks, Mary Ann," he said, beginning to waver.

"It's nice of you to ask me, and—OK, I'll come. How's Buttercup?"

"Growing like a weed, and prettier every day. I'm so glad you can come Saturday night, Tod! See you at the game!"

Usually he went to sleep the minute his head hit the pillow, but that night he was restless. The trouble with girls, he decided, was that they kept pestering you. He had been at church suppers before, but never in female company, and he was afraid he wouldn't know how to behave.

The worry gnawed at him the rest of the week, except during practice, when all his faculties were centered on football. The scrub team, fortified by Link Carey, was doing a pretty fair job with the single wing, so that the first-stringers had their hands full stopping plays.

By Friday the coach was satisfied, and he gave them no scrimmage. Flick put in an hour throwing passes to Tod and Andy, and Mike Hoban kindly waited to run Tod home in the truck.

"I'll see you around eleven o'clock tomorrow," he said in parting. "The bus leaves at noon, an' we'll have to get some lunch first. Sure hope the weather stays decent!"

Tod slept well enough, but he was awakened before dawn by the roar of wind that shook the house. The temperature had dropped, too. It looked as if they were in for a norther. As soon as breakfast was done, Tod and his father helped the hands drive the herd to shelter. Already the air was brown with blowing dust, and Tod knotted a bandanna over his mouth and nose to keep out the gritty particles, borne down on the wind from endless miles of Kansas wheat fields.

"How you expect to play football in this?" Jim Ross asked as they rode back to the house.

"It won't be fun," said Tod, "but I guess we can stand it about as well as the other team. You'd better come an' see how we make out."

"Humph!" the cattleman snorted. "I guess I'm a durn' fool, but I reckon I'll be there."

* * *

The town of Hewlett lay sprawled on the prairie, its only distinguishing landmarks the huge grain elevators by the Santa Fe tracks. The new high school had been built just outside the business section and was low and sprawling like the town.

The buses bearing the squad and the band were welcomed by the Owls' young football manager, and the boys were taken to the gym. There they were surprised to find a spacious dressing room for visiting teams, complete with showers and clothes lockers.

"Well, well," said Mike. "Some difference from the way they treated us at Logansville, huh?"

They pulled on their shoulder pads, their clean, patched jerseys and pants and socks, their scuffed football shoes.

Then as they picked up their helmets, the school bands began playing outside.

"Come on, gang," said Kleinschmidt. "Let's go out an' see how hard that wind's blowing."

They found out as soon as they left the door. The blast hit them with a force that was like a solid wall, and instantly they could feel the sting of dust in their eyes. Without waiting, they lined up and ran through some formations. At least the field was dry. Their feet got a grip on the sod instead of slipping in mud.

Across the field the Owls' orange-colored uniforms showed up brightly through the haze. And for the first time, the Cowboys had a look at a high-school team wearing face masks.

"Got to be careful how you tackle," Dutch told his squad. "If you put a hand on that mask, it's a fifteen-yard penalty!"

Prairie won the toss and lined up to receive. The wind blew dust straight across the gridiron, giving no advantage to either team. Twice the ball was toppled off the kicking tee, and finally it had to be held by an Owl lineman. The kick wasn't high, but the wind took it and blew it out of bounds. Set back five yards, it was booted once more. This time it whirled in a sidewise arc right into the arms of Chris Olsen, on the forty-yard line. The big tackle clutched it to him with a look of comical surprise, then started forward at a clumsy gallop.

"Yea, Swede!" cried the Prairie rooters, but he was tackled before he reached the midfield stripe.

They were all laughing as they gathered in the huddle. "Chris," said Joe Fortunato, "you looked like a new papa holdin' his first baby!"

"Come on—can the gab!" Flick told them. "Let's try out their line. Aaron, you carry. Right side, between guard an' tackle. Got it, everybody?"

78

The ball was snapped, the hole opened, and Weil went through for five yards. After that it was harder to gain. The Owl defense, figuring the wind made an air attack impossible, jammed into what was almost an eight-man line.

Flick looked them over coolly. "Think you can catch a pass, Tod?" he asked.

"Won't hurt to try." Tod grinned and spat out a mouthful of dust. "Just you allow for the wind," he added.

It was third down, and they were on the Hewlett forty-four. As they lined up, Tod moved out a few steps from the tackle and took off at the snap. He was all alone and a dozen yards downfield when he squinted over his shoulder into the blowing dust. The ball was coming, but it was hardly more than a dim blur. Flick had thrown five yards to his left, and the wind was curving its flight toward him. Then he had it, gripped tight in the crook of his arm, and there

was nobody near to stop him as he ran for the touchdown.

"I couldn't kick the point if I tried," said Aaron Weil in the huddle. "Give me the ball and let me go for it!"

Upset by the success of the pass, the Owls spread their defense to cover what they thought would be another. And when Mike Hoban opened a gap in the line, Weil went through like a cannonball. Suddenly, Prairie led by eight to nothing.

"Now, gang," Flick told them as they prepared to kick off, "we're going to find out about this single wing o' theirs. Let's try to keep 'em off balance! Kick it low, Aaron, an' try to angle it into the wind."

The ball flew crazily and bounced twice before it was picked up on the twenty-yard line. From there it was run back to the thirty-five behind good interference. Now came the moment of truth. Tod wondered if their week of practice would help them cope with the odd-looking formation.

From his end position he saw the long snap to the tailback and knew the play was coming his way. Ahead of the ballcarrier raced the end and two blocking backs, scowling like demons behind their fearsome masks. He saw they meant to force him in, so he dodged to the outside, brushed past the end, and dove for the man with the ball. The play was stopped for a two-yard gain.

Now they tried an off-tackle play on the opposite side, and though Andy was boxed out, Joe Luke piled up the blockers, and Aaron Weil made the tackle. It was third down and four to go. In ordinary weather that situation would surely call for a pass.

"Maybe they'll try one anyhow," Flick warned in the huddle. "But we'd better be ready for some kind of trick."

Tod saw the ball fly toward the tailback, who waited just long enough for the line to charge, then got off a punt. It was a perfectly executed quick kick, but a gust of wind swept the ball out of bounds near Prairie's thirty-yard line, where the Cowboys put it in play. Once more they started the long trek toward the opposite goal.

Through the rest of the first quarter and most of the second, there was no more scoring. Then, with the ball on the Owls' forty and only a minute to go, Flick decided to attempt another pass. He didn't send Tod out to the lonesome end spot, for there was too much danger that the wind would carry the ball over the sideline.

"Go straight down, till you're past the close-up backs," he said. "Then cut over to the right, an' I'll try to hit you."

The play went just as planned. Tod sprinted ahead to the Owls' twenty-yard stripe and swung sharply toward the sideline, looking back at Flick. The ball was on its way. Then, just as he started to reach for it, an elbow smashed across his face, and he went down in star-shot blackness.

The first thing he knew after that was that Mike's arm was around him and he was trying to sit up, spitting blood from mashed lips.

"All right, boys," said the coach's voice. "I'll take care of him. Get back in there and score!"

Dizzy and half-blind with pain, Tod was helped to his feet and guided toward the gym. Dutch Kleinschmidt supported him and talked gently as they went.

"Clear case of pass interference," he said, "and the referee caught the personal foul besides. You've got a broken nose."

They were almost at the door when a wild yell went up from the stands.

"Wha' happen'?" Tod murmured thickly.

"A touchdown, I hope. The boys'll tell us when they come in."

Tod was laid on a rubbing table, and a physician hurried in to examine his injury.

"Fracture of the septum and nose bone," Tod heard him say. "An ice pack at the back of his neck should stop the bleeding. Then I'll have to pack the nostrils. I'm afraid he's out of this game, at least, but he should be all right in another week."

Before the doctor had finished, the rest of the team came trooping in. Tired as they were, Tod heard a joyful "Yippee!" or two. Then the coach quieted them down.

"What's the score?" he asked. "Tod and I want to know."

"We made it!" said Flick. "Andy took it over on an end run. The wind spoiled the point after, though. It's fourteen to nothing. What we want to know is how Tod is."

"Outside of a smashed nose," Kleinschmidt replied, "he's OK. But he can't play any more today. Rudy, it'll be up to you."

* * *

By the time the squad left the gym again, Tod was feeling a little more like himself. There had been some rough moments when the doctor straightened the septum and thrust slabs of cotton into both nostrils. He had trouble breathing, and his head still ached. But he sat up without dizziness and gave his teammates the victory sign.

From outside, above the howl of the wind, came the shouts of spectators. But it was impossible to tell which side was being cheered. After a while he got to his feet, wrapped a blanket around him, and went out into the gale. He had been ordered to rest, so he was careful not to approach the bench or let the coach see him. At the corner of the wooden grandstand, he stood and watched the progress of the game.

Rudy Ryker was doing his best, but again and again he was boxed by the Owl end, letting the tailback sweep by for a gain. And when he was told to play farther out, the play poured through off tackle. Coupled with the vicious sting of dust on his bruised face, the sight was almost more than Tod could bear. He watched glumly until the Hewlett team

82

finally pushed the ball over, missing their try for point. Then he stumbled back into the gym, wondering how long the Cowboys could hold their lead.

Once more he lay down on the table and rested his aching head on the folded blanket. Then he must have dozed, for he was awakened by the clumping of cleated shoes.

"Shh!" somebody whispered. "Can't you see the poor guy's asleep?"

"Well," came the deeper voice of Mike Hoban, "it'll probably make him feel better to know we won!"

Tod opened his eyes. "Honest?" he croaked hoarsely. "How much?"

"Twenty to six," Flick told him. "They scored, but Andy ran back the next kickoff all the way!"

"Wow!" said Tod. "That's great!" And once more he fell back on the blanket.

"Hey!" Mike asked him. "You all right, kid?"

"Sure, just a bad headache an' a stuffed nose. Somebody want to help me dress?"

They got him bathed and into his clothes. It wasn't until he was in the bus and saw Mary Ann through the window that he remembered the church supper.

"Gosh!" he murmured to himself. "I got out of it, but I sure picked the hard way!"

9

"Man!" remarked Mike Hoban as he helped Tod into the cab of the pickup. "You got yourself the most beautiful pair o' shiners ever I saw!"

"Don't make me smile," Tod told him. "It hurts."

The force of the wind was diminishing now, but the truck was brown with dust. Mike leaned out the window to spit. "Feels as though I got half an acre of wheat field in my mouth," he said. "Did your pa come to the game?"

"I didn't see him, an' I sure hope not."

"Well," said Mike with a chuckle, "he's goin' to have a real shock when he sees that face of yours!"

Tod got out at the gate and made his way slowly to the kitchen door. As he entered, there came a scream from beside the stove. Mrs. McDonald held up her hands and stared at him.

"My land o' Goshen!" she exclaimed. "Whatever happened? Horse kick you?"

"Nope," Tod grunted. "Football game. Where's Pa?"

"One o' the men came an' got him. He had to go out to the south boundary somewhere. Steer got hung up in the barbed wire. But it's just as well he ain't here to see you—he'd have a fit!"

Tod went on into his bedroom. It was the first time he had been near a mirror since he got hurt. Now he took a look at his swollen nose and lips, his half-closed, blackened eyes, and started back with a shudder. He looked like a creature out of a horror movie.

He was resting on the bed when his father came tiptoeing in.

"You awake, son?" he whispered. "Mrs. Mack says you got bunged up some. She was right, too! Whatever happened to your face?"

"Some guy planted an elbow in it," Tod said. "But a busted nose isn't too bad. And anyhow we won the game —twenty to six!"

He managed to eat a little supper and was lying on the couch in the living room when they heard a tap at the front door. Tod's father went to open it.

"Well—hi there, Wade!" he heard him say. "Come on in. Who's this—your daughter?"

"Yep, this is our Mary Ann. How's that boy o' yours?"

Mary Ann was already across the room and kneeling by the couch. Just seeing the concern in her face gave Tod's spirits a lift.

"Don't worry," he told her, sitting up and trying to smile. "I'm OK now. Mighty sorry I had to miss the church sup- per, though."

"I left as soon as I could," she said. "I brought you some cupcakes I made myself. Oh, Tod! You look so terrible! Are you sure the doctor did all he could?"

"Oh, sure, I reckon so. He seemed to know his business. Honest, Mary Ann, I hoped you wouldn't have to see me like this, but I'm going to be fine. By next Saturday I'll be back in uniform—maybe playing."

"Great!" she said. "I hope you're right. You've made a winner out of the team this year."

"Me? Gosh, no! It's Flick an' Andy an' Mike. They'd get

on fine without me. Sorry I can't talk better. My nose is full o' cotton."

"I know," she told him. "It must be just awful. Well, we have to go now, but I hope you like the little cakes!"

After they had gone, Tod's father looked at him quizzically. "Seems to me Wade Foster's girl sort o' likes you," he said. "That's all right. She's a nice youngster—pretty, too. Tell me, do you really think you'll be playin' by a week from now?"

"Sure—why not? It's not like a busted arm or leg. If I can see to catch passes, I'll be in there."

As he found out during the next six days, a broken nose is slow to mend. He went back to school on Monday and visited the family doctor that noon. But all that could be done was to repack the nostrils and apply a wide plaster patch across the bridge of the nose. Tod's blackened eyes had faded to a sickly green, but he still spoke like a boy with a bad head cold.

In the old days his schoolmates would have left him alone. Now they were not only kind but also anxious for his recovery. That, he realized wryly, was what came of being on the football team. It made him a little angry that he should be given special treatment on that account.

By Tuesday he donned his uniform and started practice, though the coach didn't let him take part in the scrimmage. The scrubs had gone back to their customary T formation as the team prepared to meet the Caine Coyotes at home. Caine was known as a tricky and resourceful outfit.

"They aren't any bigger than we are," Coach Kleinschmidt told the squad. "But they have fast backs and may come up with some fancy plays. We'll have to be on our toes every minute."

Tod did some running to keep his legs in condition, and the coach assigned one of the smaller boys with a good arm to throw him a lot of passes. At first he found it hard to focus

86

his eyes on the ball, but after half an hour he could see it coming without trouble. And his hands were as sure as ever.

The weather had turned fair and warm after the norther. "I'd sure like to play our next game on a day like this," said Mike as they drove home. "We've durn' near drowned, an' we've had our mouths full o' dust. Be good to get back to plain old football!"

"I guess you never can tell," Tod answered. "Kansas weather can change overnight, an' generally does."

On the ranch the stock had been driven back to the lower end of the range, where the pasture was still good. In another month, Tod knew, the steers would be heavy enough to ship east to the Kansas City market. For his father's sake, he hoped that beef prices would stay up.

After supper Jim Ross was reading the news while Tod did his homework. Suddenly, he slapped the paper down with an angry crackle.

"Son," he said, "what about this Caine team? They as good as some folks seem to think? This sports writer says they'll win the Tri-County championship, now that they've beaten Wykoff."

The boy laughed. "Quit worrying, Pa," he replied. "Caine's lost one game, same as we have. All I can tell you is we'll give 'em all we've got. Sure, I guess they're pretty good. But so are we."

On Friday, when Tod reported at the gym, Dutch Kleinschmidt had a surprise for him.

"Here," said the coach. "Try this on and see if you like it."

What he handed him was a brand-new helmet with a face guard attached. Tod put it on gingerly and felt the two stout bars that crossed his face just beyond his bandaged nose. The mask wasn't as heavy as he expected, and, more important, it didn't block his vision.

"Golly!" he said. "You must have paid a lot for this. Think I really need it?"

Kleinschmidt chuckled. "Don't bother yourself about the cost," he said. "Somebody gave me the money. What I want to know is how it feels. Can you see all right?"

"Sure—I think so. Have to try it out 'fore I know. But it feels OK. Doesn't seem to weigh any more'n my old helmet."

"Good. Come on out and let me throw you a couple."

The first pass was a high floater that Tod caught without trouble. Then the coach pitched a bullet. It came on a line, and he had to jump high to take it. But as far as he could tell, the face mask hadn't bothered him in the least.

"That's fine!" Dutch commented. "Now I won't have to worry about your getting that nose mashed again."

The other members of the team stood around admiring the new equipment, some of them with envy. Several wanted to try it on.

"Maybe next year," the coach told them, "there'll be enough cash in the athletic fund so you can all wear 'em. I'd like to get new uniforms, too, but right now we've got to win our games in the old outfits."

When Saturday morning dawned, Tod jumped out of bed for a look at the sunrise. It was a crisp, clear autumn day with hardly a breath of wind. Perfect football weather! He dressed and did his morning chores, then came in to breakfast.

"I'd like about four o' those eggs, Mrs. Mack," he told the housekeeper. "Got to pile in enough energy to last me through the game!"

"Sure your nose'll be all right?" his father asked.

"No chance of any trouble now," Tod replied. "I've got a new helmet with a face guard. You won't recognize me if you're there. Mike says it makes me look like a Green Bay Packer!"

88

His father made no comment. He merely nodded, and his face disappeared behind his coffee cup.

*   *   *

"We kick off to them," said Kleinschmidt to the squad assembled in front of the bench. "Rudy, you'll start at right end on defense. I'll save Tod until we have the ball. All right, boys—get out there and show 'em!"

Tod wrapped a blanket around himself and sat down beside the coach. The Caine Coyotes were talking it up as they prepared to receive. A pretty good-looking bunch, he thought, in their scarlet-and-white uniforms. Then he leaned forward tensely to watch the kick sail downfield. One of the two deep men caught it neatly on the twelve and started across, dodging tacklers. Then the other back sprinted behind him, taking a behind-the-back pass-off and setting sail for the opposite side of the field. With most of the Cowboys drawn off to the right, he ran it all the way to the forty before Flick Davis nailed him.

The red-shirts were riding high. They lined up with swift precision, and on a quick count a pass was thrown out into the flat. An end took it on the run and sped for a first down in Prairie territory. Kleinschmidt frowned, and though he said nothing, Tod knew what he was thinking. The gain had been made around Rudy Ryker's end.

On the theory that a good play should be repeated, the Coyotes tried it again, this time to the opposite side. Andy Willis, expecting just that, had moved out a little to his left, and he was there to slap the pass down before it could be caught.

"All right," said Dutch, more to himself than to Todd, "so now what'll they do?"

With second down and ten, the fullback slammed into the line and was stopped after a three-yard gain. Tod inched forward nervously on the bench, watching Rudy. He was sure the play would come to the big end's side, and he was right. It was another flare pass, caught just before the runner reached the line of scrimmage. But Rudy, moving with surprising speed, flung out his big arms and tackled the man in his tracks. A happy cheer rose from the Prairie fans, for everybody liked Rudy.

The coach's frown had given place to a grin. "Fourth down!" he exclaimed. "Get loosened up, Tod. You'll go in after they punt."

Tod pranced up and down the sideline, swung his arms and was ready. The kick was deep, and Andy could barely make the twenty on his runback. Immediately Tod ran on the field, and Rudy came back to the bench.

Flick called two plays into the line for short gains. Then,

on third down with two to go, he shot a pass to Andy Willis, who made a solid fifteen yards. It was first down and well past the forty.

In the huddle Flick outlined the next play. "I reckon they'll expect a buck," he said. "I'll fake to Aaron an' pass to you, Tod. Not too long—just past the linebackers."

Tod nodded and lined up, a few yards out from Mike Hoban. At the snap he was off, trotting easily past the Coyote end, who seemed intent on the Prairie line. The secondary defense had seen what looked like a hand-off to the fullback and were charging in that direction. Then Flick's pass came out to Tod, straight and true. He made the catch and was on his way.

The freshly whitened chalk lines flashed past under his galloping feet. At first he felt light and strong. When the

safety man roared in for the tackle, he offered him a hip, swiveled away, and sprinted on. The pounding of feet behind him faded. He was over the last stripe!

But once the touchdown was made, he suddenly stumbled and sat down. His lungs felt as if they would burst, and he lay there like a fish out of water, gasping for air. Dimly he wondered how he could have gotten so badly out of condition. Then it came to him. He had been running at full speed with a tightly plugged nose, forced to breathe through his mouth!

When Flick came to help him up, he managed to grin. "Don't—ask me to—run again—for a while!" he panted. "Can't breathe!"

"All right," the quarterback told him. "Let's get back to the bench, an' I'll ask Dutch to put Rudy in."

The second-stringers greeted him as a hero, and the coach helped put the blanket around his heaving shoulders.

"Sorry, Tod," he said. "I should have had more sense. But you made a beautiful run, breath or no breath."

Aaron Weil's well-trained toe made the score seven to nothing, and the Cowboys kicked off again. A good runback put the Caine team in business on the thirty-five-yard line, and at once they tried a long pass. It almost succeeded. Only a last-second effort by Flick, at safety, batted it out of the receiver's hands.

They made a first down by rushing and then attempted another pass that was caught well down toward Prairie's end of the field. Joe Luke made the tackle. He hit the ball-carrier so hard that there was a fumble, and Weil made the recovery, to a bedlam of yells from the excited Prairie fans.

"Look, coach," Tod pleaded, "I'm fine now. Can't I go back in?"

"Not yet," Kleinschmidt told him. "You get some more rest. We may need you later."

The Cowboys were lining up on their own eighteen. Two

92

plunges by the fullback took them to the twenty-five, and a pitchout to Andy made another eight yards for a first down. Just as the next play started, Tod felt a hand on his shoulder.

"What's the matter, boy?" he heard his father's rough voice. "You get hurt again? Just tell me who did it!"

10

Tod chuckled. "I'm OK, Pa, an' nobody laid a hand on me. You know Dutch Kleinschmidt, our coach. He'll tell you everything's all right."

"It is," said Dutch, shaking hands. "He just sprinted about sixty yards for a touchdown, and since he couldn't breathe right, he got pretty badly winded. I'll be sending him in again if he's needed."

"Good," the cattleman answered with relief. "When I got here, all I saw was Tod on the ground an' didn't know what happened. How's the score look?"

Dutch was up, trying to get Flick's attention, so Tod answered. "Right now we're ahead, seven to nothing, but we don't seem to be making the gains we should. Let's watch it an' see."

It was third down and six yards to go, and the Coyote defense was spreading out, in the certain expectation of a forward pass. Tod leaned forward, intent on the way the team lined up. Mike Hoban, he saw with surprise, was out of position, a full two yards back of the other men in the line.

At the snap of the ball, the ends hustled down the field and the Caine linebackers ran with them. Flick was in the pocket, taking his time, Then, to Tod's amazement, the ball was tossed high and short, directly over the charging line, where the only visible Prairie player was the big right tackle. Mike took the pass, tucked it under his arm, and went galloping on.

The coach watched the play gain twenty yards and turned back to the bench with a grin. He saw the look of unbelief on Tod's face.

"It's all right," he explained. "A tackle-eligible formation we've had up our sleeve, and it worked!"

The Coyote captain was protesting violently to the officials, but he lost the argument. Both the referee and the head linesman had watched the formation and assured the irate red-shirts that it was perfectly legal.

When the excitement died down, the Cowboys went to work once more. Another hard-earned first down put the ball on the Caine forty-five, and Dutch beckoned to Tod.

"Here goes, Pa!" he said as he tossed off his blanket. "Wish me luck!"

The first play was an off-tackle smash by Joe Luke, with Tod taking out the opposing end. It went for seven yards, and as the team lined up again, the right end was standing inconspicuously near the sideline.

"Hey—what you doin' over here?" came his father's grating voice, and Tod felt his face flush crimson.

Flick made a quick call and got his pass away before the Coyotes could react. Tod barely got his hands up in time to make the catch. Then he was away, cutting inside a tackler who was rushing toward the side boundary. He had no blockers, but he straight-armed one back and sped on. Finally the safety man overtook him at the five-yard line. Again he was breathing hard when he surrendered the ball to the referee, but he got his wind back in the huddle.

"Take it easy, Tod," Flick told him. "This'll be 'round the left side."

With Andy and Chris Olsen blocking for him, Tony Fortunato carried to the one. And from there, behind the hard-charging Link Carey, Flick dove across the goal line.

"What do you say, gang?" he asked in the huddle. "Want to make it a two-pointer?"

They all agreed, and a flare pass to Andy did the trick. The Prairie lead had climbed to fifteen. There was no more scoring during the rest of the half, for the Cowboys put up a stone-wall defense.

They rested during half time, stretched out on benches in the locker room. Tod was the only one who felt fresh and ready to go, and he begged the coach to let him start.

It was the Coyotes' turn to kick off, and Prairie would receive, so Dutch told Tod to go ahead out with the team. The kick was a crazy one, low and bounding. Pancho Villa tried to grab it on first bounce, but it slid off his fingers. Suddenly there was a frantic pile-up, and when the referee had unscrambled it, he gestured toward the Prairie goal. Caine had recovered!

Fired up by the break, the Coyotes made two successive first downs that put them on the eight-yard line. An end sweep around Tod's end was stopped, but a quick pass over center reached the one. From there the Coyote fullback bulled it over. The placement kick was good, and Caine had seven points.

"I'll bet it's an onside kick!" Flick told them as they huddled before receiving the kickoff. "That last one would give 'em ideas. You guys up front get ready for it!"

There was nothing unusual about the way the ball was set up on the tee, but when the kicker approached it, Tod saw him veer and come in from the side. As his toe met the leather, the ball popped up, sailing to the right, high over Tod's head. He didn't try to reach for it, for a touch might deflect it and make it a free ball. Instead, he watched it bobble over the sideline. Caine had to take it back and kick again from their own thirty-five.

There was no onside kick this time. The ball sailed high, and Andy, surrounded by Coyotes, made a fair catch on the Prairie thirty. The Caine squad boasted enough men for a two-platoon system, so the defensive team was relatively fresh. Against their determined charge, the tired Cowboys had all they could do to make a first down. Flick tried passes to Tod and to Andy, but both were covered too closely. Then the quarterback was blitzed and had to eat the ball, back on his own thirty. It was fourth down now and long yardage to go.

Under pressure, Aaron Weil got off a punt that was caught and run back almost to midfield. And a hungry Coyote offensive team came racing onto the gridiron.

"Hold that line! Hold that line!" screamed the Prairie cheering section.

"All right, gang, you heard 'em," said Flick grimly. "You can do it!"

The linemen gave ground grudgingly, but one first down was made, and then another. Tod had been taken out and Ryker put in on defense. With a third down and three on the twenty-yard line, the Coyotes pulled an end-around play that fooled Rudy completely. The ballcarrier ran to the five before Flick could knock him out of bounds. From there it took just three plays to punch it over.

With the score fifteen to thirteen in Prairie's favor, the visiting team wasn't going to settle for a one-pointer. They lined up in regular formation, and the quarterback threw a pass. It would have been good, except that it was caught a full step beyond the end zone. The Cowboys still had their slender two-point lead.

There was a time-out while the Caine defensive unit came in for the kickoff.

"Listen, now," said Flick, "and listen hard. Those guys think they've got us on the run. There's ten minutes left to play, and if they hold us, as they're sure they can, they expect to make another touchdown."

"OK," growled big Mike Hoban, "let's cross 'em up—let's score!"

"Why not?" said Tod, who had just been sent in. "I know you guys are bushed, but I've had a lot o' rest. Throw me one, Flick, an' I'll prove it!"

The quarterback nodded. "First play after we receive, stay out there at split end. I'll give a fast count an' throw wherever you are."

Once more the ball was teed up, and once more Caine tried an onside kick. It traveled the required ten yards and would have worked perfectly if Joe Luke hadn't anticipated it. He had moved up from his regular post, and now he dove on the rolling oval with a pounce like a bobcat. It was Prairie's ball on their own forty-five.

Tod didn't join the huddle but stayed out on the wing, trying to make himself invisible. Then a defensive back spotted him, just as Flick was starting to call signals.

"Look out!" he yelled, but the ball had been snapped, and Tod was on his way. He sprinted ahead ten or fifteen yards before he looked over his shoulder. The ball was coming, but so was the Coyote cornerback. They went up for it almost together, and it was Tod's strong fingers that held it. Then the back tackled him viciously, grabbing first at his arm, then at his face mask. Tod felt the wrench in his neck and stumbled, falling forward but still gripping the football.

Above him he heard the referee's whistle, then a hard voice reprimanding the Caine defenseman. As he got to his feet, he saw a fifteen-yard penalty being paced off against the Coyotes. It placed the ball on their twenty-one-yard line.

"You hurt, Tod?" asked Flick in worried tones. "That so-an'-so really jerked your mask around."

"I thought he'd break my neck." Tod laughed. "But I'm fine now. Let's get that touchdown!"

98

"OK. You take out the end, and we'll send Aaron off tackle."

Tod braced his feet and waited for the snap of the ball. Then he met the Coyote's left end with a solid block and ran on to get the linebacker as well. Mike had taken care of the opposing tackle. Aaron Weil wasn't fast, but he weighed a hundred and ninety and ran with his knees high. It usually took two tacklers to bring him down. This time there was nobody but the safety man, and the big fullback literally carried him for an extra five yards. The ball was on Caine's six-yard line.

"Hit 'em again! Hit 'em again! Har-*der!* Har-*der!*" chanted the Prairie cheering section.

Another crack at the line netted only a yard. "We'll never make it that way," said Flick in the huddle. "Let's go for it right now with a pass. Andy an' Tod, both o' you cut for the corners. I'll throw to whichever one's open."

Tod thought fast. He might draw off the defensive backs if he acted like the intended receiver. So he took his position ten yards out and made a show of digging his cleats into the dirt. Flick barked out the signals, took the snap, and ran back to escape the blitzing line. Tod, on the goal line, yelled, waved his arms invitingly, and succeeded in attracting the attention of the Coyotes' defense. And Andy, scuttling across into his corner of the end zone, took Flick's easy pass for a touchdown.

Jubilantly they came back into the huddle. "Thanks, pal!" said Andy with a grin, and slapped Tod on the back. They lined up in a solid wall to protect the placement, and the dependable Weil put it over the bar. The score was twenty-two to thirteen.

It seemed as if that touchdown had given the Cowboys their second wind. They charged harder on the defense, and the Coyotes could make only one first down before they were forced to kick. From that point on, the game was all

Prairie's. They were well into enemy territory when the final gun sounded.

Jim Ross drove his son home after he had showered and dressed.

"I was right proud o' you, Tod," he remarked, and Tod, who rarely heard any words of praise at home, was more pleased than he liked to show.

"Maybe I'll do better when I can breathe right," he said. "The Doc promised to take the packing out o' my nose this week. But that face mask was a big help—made me feel safer."

He stole a look at his father, but the older man's face was as expressionless as a wooden Indian's.

On Sunday morning Tod slept an extra hour, and when he came down at seven-thirty, his father was gone.

"Where'd Pa get to?" he asked Mrs. McDonald.

"Said he had to go to town. But you ain't to wait breakfast for him. Here's your orange juice. How many pancakes you reckon you can eat?"

Tod laughed. "You know me. Just keep making 'em!"

While he was working on his second stack, he heard the car drive in. His father entered, carrying the Sunday paper and wearing a pleased expression on his rugged face.

"That sports-writin' feller," he commented, "is gettin' some sense."

"Why—what's he say now?"

"Thinks maybe it'll be a hot race for the Tri-County championship. Three teams, maybe four, have got a chance. An' Prairie's one of 'em.

"That ain't all—listen to this: 'When the Prairie Cowboys took the measure of a strong Caine team by 22 to 13 today, football fans in western Kansas realized there was a new high-school grid power rising in their midst. Dutch Kleinschmidt has put together a well-drilled squad, with one of the best passing quarterbacks around and a couple

100

of ends any coach would like to have. Prairie is a small school and thin on replacements, but the boys seem to be rugged enough to play both ways.' "

"Gee!" said Tod. "That sounds pretty good. You suppose he was there?"

"Nope. But if we keep on winnin' games, he'll come. Here's the list o' teams in the Tri-County, an' how they stand now. Prairie an' Skipton are tied, with four wins an' one loss. Then come Caine an' Wykoff an' Lundy—won three an' lost two. Rowell's only won one game out o' five, an' you play 'em this week. Ought to be easy."

"Maybe," Tod replied, "but I guess nobody's really easy in this league. Besides, it'll be on their home grounds. I wouldn't take any game for granted."

On Monday, at skull practice in the gymnasium, Dutch Kleinschmidt used almost the same words. "I hope you boys haven't been reading the papers," he said. "If anyone here thinks we can coast in from here, he'd better not say so where I can hear him. Rowell and Prairie have been rivals for a lot of years, and they've never been easy to beat. This time they'll be playing at home. And some of you may remember that quarterback of theirs—Hook Jones. He was hurt when they lost their first three games. Now he's back in the lineup, and you'll notice they trimmed Juliana Saturday.

"So I'm telling you, we can't let down for this one. Tomorrow I'm going to give you a stiff scrimmage, and you'll keep it up all week."

They went outside to jog a few laps around the field and loosen up.

"Aw, heck!" Tod heard the guard, Pancho Villa, complain. "I was lookin' forward to a nice, easy week. What do we have to work so much for? Rowell ought to be a cinch."

Flick Davis heard him, too. "Pancho," he said, "you figure you're overworked or something? I'd like to think the boys over at Rowell look at it the way you do—that they're licked before they start. But if I know Hook Jones, he an' his coach are busy right now, dreamin' up ways to beat us. Come on —race you to the other end o' the field!"

Perhaps he imagined it, but Tod had a persistent idea that others on the squad felt like Pancho. They kidded more than usual, and if they thought the coach wasn't looking, they sometimes missed their assignments in practice. After going to the doctor's office Monday noon, Tod was rid of the bothersome nose pads and eager to play football. So the lackadaisical attitude of some of the boys irked him.

Waiting for Mike after practice on Wednesday, he was standing near the gym door. Moodily he scowled and kicked at pebbles.

"Hi, Tod!" said a voice at his elbow. "Why the thunderclouds? Something wrong?"

He looked up and saw Mary Ann. "Nothing I can do much about," he told her. "Some o' the guys on the squad aren't taking this Rowell game seriously—that's all. An' I'd sure hate to lose that one!"

She nodded. "I can tell the students have let down, too," she said. "I wanted to organize a big pep rally for Friday night, and know what? The other yell leaders said they'd rather go to the movies!"

"Gee!" said Tod with disgust. "It was a swell idea, anyhow. Why don't you go ahead—put up the posters—get the kids to bring wood for a bonfire. Maybe we can still wake everybody up!"

11

Mary Ann must have worked like a beaver, for on Friday there were rally posters everywhere. In an open lot next to the athletic field, old boards, broken boxes, and barrels had been gathered and piled up, ready to be lighted. Some enterprising youngster had even climbed up the water tank and painted BEAT ROWELL in letters six feet high.

For his part, Tod had persuaded Coach Kleinschmidt and the co-captains, Flick Davis and Mike Hoban, to appear at the rally and say a few words. It had to be held at seven-thirty in the evening, so that all members of the squad could get to bed early, but it was dark enough for the fire by then.

Drawn by curiosity and the red glow in the sky, nearly all the Prairie student body showed up. Mary Ann danced out, silhouetted against the fire, and started things off by calling for a long yell for the team. Then followed "Yippee-ki-yis" for every man on the starting eleven. By that time the youngsters were showing some enthusiasm, and they cheered without urging when Dutch Kleinschmidt stepped out to speak.

"When I first took this coaching job," he said, "I was told that only one game counted. We might lose all the rest, but if we could beat the Rowell Raiders, the season would be a success. We managed to do it that year. But then came two seasons when Rowell trimmed us. They lost some seniors last spring, and they've run into a losing streak. But I know this—there's one game they mean to win. That's the game with us. This minute I understand there's a parade marching up the main street in Rowell. They've got three bands playing, and all the banners say, 'Beat Prairie!' Tomorrow they'll be on their home field, and they'll be out for blood. That's why the team needs every one of you in the stand, letting us know you're behind us!"

Flick echoed the coach's sentiments and admitted he was frankly worried about a letdown. "We've had a lot of lucky breaks so far this fall," he said. "Let's not get the idea we're good. Our wins have come from luck and from trying extra hard."

All Mike Hoban said was, "Don't think those Raiders'll be easy! They'll be up for this one—and we'd better be!"

Tod was sorry not to see more of the squad at the rally. Those who were there were obviously shaken a bit in their complacency, and he wished all of them had been present. Mike had driven him back to town after supper, and now he rode home with the big tackle.

"I wish this game was over," said Tod. "I've got a funny feeling about it."

"Yep," Mike grunted. "I know what you mean."

*　*　*

It was cold that Saturday, windy and cloudy. The wind wasn't a gale, but it came in gusts, first from one direction, then from another. Weather predictions called for rain, but at game time it still held off.

"Come on, gang!" called Flick when they were dressed. "Let's get out there an' show 'em!"

There was something disheartening to Tod in the way they strolled out, more in a mood for joking and horseplay than for victory. In the stands, however, there seemed to be

104

more spirit. The pep rally had keyed up the Prairie students, and a lot of them were there. Their cheers came strong to greet the team. Across the field some four hundred rabid Rowell fans answered them cheer for cheer.

The Raiders snapped into their drill. Their orange-and-blue jerseys and orange helmets brightened up the cloudy day. And when the coin was tossed, the Raiders won, choosing to kick off, which surprised everybody.

It was a high kick. At the top of its arc one of those errant gusts of wind took it and blew it away from Andy Willis. The ball bounded along toward the goal line but didn't go over. A Rowell play had downed it just a yard short.

Prairie was in a hole already, and the game was only seconds old. In the huddle Flick tried to put some spunk into his disorganized teammates.

"Come on, you guys," he snapped. "Open a hole in that line so Aaron can get us out o' here!"

They lined up with their feet right on the goal stripe as Flick called signals. Then, one of the few times in his life, Link Carey made a bad pass to the quarterback. Flick grabbed up the bobbled ball, but a hard-charging guard tackled him behind the line for a safety. Two points went up on the scoreboard for the home team, and their cheering section went crazy. On the Prairie side there was stupefied silence.

Safeties were something new to most of the Cowboys, and the next procedure bewildered them. The referee explained the rule. They would have to kick from their twenty-yard line.

"It's all right, Flick," Link Carey promised solemnly. "I'll give Aaron a good pass this time."

They lined up in punt formation, and immediately the overeager Raiders gave them a break by jumping offside. The five-yard penalty gave them room to maneuver, and it gave them time to gather their wits. The linemen braced themselves, the pass went back perfectly, and Aaron's foot sent the ball sailing better than fifty yards downfield. The fair catch made by Rowell's deep man gave the visitors a first down on their own thirty.

Dutch Kleinschmidt took Tod out and sent big Rudy Ryker in on defense. Hardly had Tod wrapped himself in his blanket when play started. Hook Jones took the snap without calling any signals, ran back to fake a pass, and when the defense broke through to blitz him, he was no longer there. With two backfield men running interference, he sprinted around the Cowboys' right end and made nearly twenty yards. Rudy had been forced completely out of the play.

Tod didn't say anything, but he knew the coach was disturbed. "Get up," he growled, "and be ready to go in again."

Rowell was at midfield now, and the next play took them even deeper into Prairie territory. It was a smartly executed jump pass over center to the left end, who had drifted across and in. He took the ball for another first down on the thirty-five.

A line plunge advanced it six more yards, and the Prairie line dug in, expecting a repetition. Tod was sure the crafty Jones would cross them up with a pass, and he was right. The quarterback faked a convincing hand-off to the full-back, then ran back a few steps and heaved a long one. Flick was there to cover, but the wind took the ball. It bounced off his fingers into the hands of a Rowell receiver, and in two strides he had a touchdown. When the Raiders kicked the point after, they led by nine to nothing.

Tod was sent in to replace Ryker again, and the team lined up to receive. In their faces he saw a kind of dull disbelief. They were taking a licking from one of the "easy" opponents on their schedule, and the thought of it was hard to digest.

Andy Willis took the kickoff on the fifteen and started his

106

runback. But the blocking ahead of him fell apart. He could only reach the twenty-yard line.

"All right, now," said Flick in the huddle. "Don't get upset. Pull up your pants an' let's go! We'll try Luke off tackle first—a thirty-two play."

The halfback nodded, and they lined up. But Pancho Villa pulled the unpardonable boner of starting offside. The five-yard penalty made it first and fifteen.

"Come—steady up, you guys!" Flick urged. "I've got to pass now, so give me some protection. It'll be to you, Tod—down and out."

Tod was ready. Off at the snap, he sprinted downfield for twenty yards, then toward the sideline. But when he looked for the ball, all he saw was a pileup behind the line of scrimmage. Flick had been swarmed under before he could throw. Even worse, he had lost the ball or had it wrestled out of his arms. The referee was standing on the Cowboys' ten and pointing vigorously in the direction of their goal. Tod rejoined the team as they lined up slowly on defense. The next Raider play was a sweep around Tod's end, and he took out the lead blocker, rolled to his feet, and made the tackle before the ballcarrier could cross the line of scrimmage.

"Hold that line! Hold that line!" came a ragged chant from the Prairie stand. But the Rowell attack had hardly been slowed. In two vicious plunges they slammed over for another touchdown. The point after was missed, but the score stood at fifteen to nothing in the Raiders' favor.

There was a bitter taste in Tod's mouth as he watched his teammates straggle to their positions to receive the kickoff. They were a bunch of quitters, he thought. The famous Cowboys! He had heard that once, years ago, the nickname of the team had been the "Prairie Chickens." Then the word "chicken" came to have a bad connotation, and it was changed to "Prairie Cowboys." Anyhow, he was almost ashamed to be one of them today.

Andy Willis, at least, was still trying. He took the ball on the twenty-two and zigzagged through would-be tacklers for twenty yards, almost single-handed. Flick Davis faced the huddle grimly.

"Andy came here to play football," he told them. "How about the rest of you? We're going to make a first down now if I have to carry the ball myself. Snap to it, you linemen, and open up some holes!"

He sent Joe Luke off tackle on the right side, and Mike Hoban charged hard, piling up two men, while Tod took out the end. Luke made it across midfield and was only a yard short of a first down. "Quick, now," Flick told the team. "Hit 'em again!"

This time Aaron Weil carried, plowing ahead for five yards. And on the next play Tod caught a line-drive pass on the thirty, reaching the enemy's twenty-yard line before he was brought down.

The end of the quarter was called, and both teams trotted to the other end of the field. As he passed the Prairie rooting section, Tod saw Mary Ann pleading with the fans for more pep in their cheering. Then he was in the huddle again, and Flick called for a shotgun formation.

"I want at least three receivers out there," he said. "And I hope they try to cover you all!"

Possibly the Raiders had never seen the shotgun before. When Flick took his place ten yards behind the center, the defending backs did a lot of yelling and scurrying around. They even left a five-man line and pulled both ends back to cover pass receivers.

Flick got the ball from Carey, held it high as if looking for a clear target, and suddenly started to run. Joe Luke took out the first tackler in his path. Then Tod blocked another back. And Flick came streaking on, hugging the sideline. He was over for a touchdown before most of the defenders knew what was happening.

108

"Let's go for two!" he panted in the huddle. "I'll pass to you, Andy." He flipped one to the split left end. Andy made it, running like a jackrabbit.

The Prairie fans had something to cheer about at last, and their sustained yelling seemed to help the team keep its new-found momentum. Rowell had to fight harder for first downs now, and after a long, slow advance to the fifty-yard line, they were forced to punt.

When the half ended, Prairie was well down in Raider country, but the score still remained fifteen to eight in Rowell's favor.

It was pretty quiet in the locker room. Not so much, Tod thought, because the boys were tired, as that they had little to brag about. Dutch Kleinschmidt walked slowly back and forth in front of them. He looked serious but not angry. Finally he began to speak.

"Every team has a letdown once in a while. It happens to the best—even the Colts—the Rams—the Packers. The thing I'd planned to say to you was that a really good team never stops trying. You went into this game with a chance to have the best record in the league. Maybe some of you thought you had it already and didn't need to work. What they did to you in those first ten minutes was just what you deserved. Now it looks as if you may have learned your lesson. So all I'm going to tell you is one thing. The team that comes out of this on top will be the one that never quits. I don't mind losing to a better team. What I can't bear is to see you licked for want of an honest effort."

On the field the gusty wind still blew fitfully, and the sky had darkened. It was Prairie's turn to kick to Rowell. Tod, lining up, was glad to see the sober faces of the team and the businesslike way they took their positions, while the cheers still echoed from the stands. The coach had let him play defense, which also pleased him. Weil booted a low, hard one that traveled to the fifteen and was run back ten yards.

Hook Jones gathered his men in the huddle. It was when they came out of it to line up that Tod had an uneasy feeling. He didn't like the excited grin on the face of the end opposite him.

"Hey—look out for a trick!" he yelled, and braced himself for trouble. Then, almost before the words were out of his mouth, the play had started. He saw Jones drop back, arm raised with the ball. But the end didn't dash upfield to catch the pass. Instead, he charged straight at Tod, in an effort to take him out. Meanwhile, the Cowboys were clawing through the line to get at the passer. Tod sidestepped the end's rush and kept his eye on the quarterback. Suddenly he realized that the ball had vanished. The right end, running behind Jones, was making a sweep around Tod's side of the line, with the flanker-back running interference.

Tod had never seen or heard of the "Statue of Liberty" play, but he knew he had to stop that ballcarrier. He gave the blocking back a shoulder and went on without losing stride. The man with the ball was fast. Skirting the side boundary, he was close to the line of scrimmage, and not a Prairie player was there to bar his way. Tod sprinted diagonally across and launched a dive that bumped the ballcarrier out of bounds. If he had been a split second later, the man would have been touchdown-bound. As it was, he was three yards short of a first down.

"Where'd he come from?" Flick Davis asked. "I was lookin' for a pass. Lucky thing you nailed him, Tod! Come on, gang—stop 'em again!"

12

The failure of their great trick play seemed to take some of the fire out of the Raiders. They sent a plunge at the line that was stopped for no gain. And with a third down and three, Hook Jones tossed a long pass. It went over the intended receiver's head and landed right in Flick Davis's outstretched hands. He reached the Rowell forty-five before he was tackled.

The Prairie rooters had been yelling, "Get that ball!" Now they changed the chant to, "We want a touchdown!"

The team wanted one, too. Their determination was evident in the way they charged. Two first downs were made on straight line bucks by Weil and Luke. Then, with the ball on the eighteen, Flick told Tod to get ready for a "ninety" play. After a short gain, Tod drifted out slowly to his lonesome end spot without being noticed. At the snap he was away, racing down the sideline, and Flick found him with a perfectly timed pass. He caught it on the two-yard line and went over with a tackler hanging on his back.

The yelling was so loud that Flick could barely be heard in the huddle. "Want to tie it?" he asked. "Or shall we take a chance an' try to go a point ahead?"

They all voted for a two-point try, and the pass flew toward Andy Willis. It was a trifle high. The little end made a valiant leap, but the ball slid off his fingertips. The score remained fifteen to fourteen in the Raiders' favor, and a groan went up from the Prairie crowd.

"All right, gang," said Flick. "We gambled and didn't make it. That was my fault. So now we start fresh. Hold 'em, line, an' get that ball!"

Rowell started on the twenty after a long kick went over the goal line. With a one-point lead to protect, they moved slowly, trying to use up time. The Prairie team, on the other hand, tore in like a pack of hungry wolves. Twice they flattened Hook Jones before he could get a pass away. And when the hometowners finally had to punt, they blocked so well for Andy Willis that the little sprinter ran the kick back for forty yards.

From there it was only a matter of minutes till they had their third touchdown, and as they picked up momentum, the Raiders began to fall apart. In the last quarter Prairie scored again. With a twenty-eight to fifteen lead, Dutch Kleinschmidt started substituting, and it was the scrub team that held Rowell scoreless through the final minutes. Sitting on the bench, the varsity players cheered till their throats were hoarse.

Tod and Mike took their showers, dressed, and came out of the gym together. To their surprise a delegation was waiting there—the three girl cheerleaders and a small crowd of faithful fans.

"We knew you could do it!" cried Mary Ann. "Never mind what happened in that first quarter—we knew you'd come back!" And in a sudden excess of school spirit, she flung her arms around both boys and hugged them.

"Hey!" Mike laughed. "We weren't that good! Matter of fact, we should have been slapped for the way we played."

"Right!" Tod agreed. "Save it for a couple more weeks an' see if we deserve it."

He didn't see his father till he got home. The cattleman's greeting was gruff.

"Well, how bad did you get licked?" he asked.

"I thought you were there," Tod told him. "Didn't you stay till the end?"

"Nope. Left after the first two touchdowns. Never could stand a bunch o' boys that'd give up when things went wrong."

"Can't say I blame you," his son replied. "Some of us were overconfident. But if you'd stuck it out, you'd have seen a different game. We played our heads off in the second half. Beat 'em twenty-eight to fifteen."

"Hm! Yep—guess I shoulda stayed. Understand, boy, I wasn't talkin' about you personally. Near as I could tell, you were doin' all you could. Anyhow, it's good to hear the rest of 'em snapped out of it."

It appeared, when they read the Sunday paper the next day, that the sportswriter sent to cover the game had also left early. The score was given correctly, but most of the write-up was a scathing criticism of high-school players who thought they could win without trying.

"If the Prairie Cowboys had their swelled heads reduced in the Rowell game," it concluded, "they might really get somewhere in the Tri-County League."

Studying the standings of the eight teams, Tod found that only Skipton had a record to equal Prairie's. Both schools had now won five and lost one. They would be facing each other in the final game, and it was to be played on the Cowboys' home field! But first, he remembered soberly, they had to beat another tough team—the Lundy Longhorns—who sported a four and two record.

"How are the steers coming, Pa?" he asked. "Must be 'most ready to ship, aren't they?"

"They're still puttin' on weight," his father answered.

"Won't hurt to give 'em a few more pounds. I figure I'll send 'em to market in a week or two."

There were nearly two hundred blocky Herefords in the feed lot. The hands spent most of their time keeping the feeding cribs filled with corn and the troughs with water. Now the animals were nearing the desired weight of close to a thousand pounds apiece. When the time came, they would be trucked to the Santa Fe pens in Prairie and put aboard the cattle cars that would take them to the Kansas City stockyards. With luck they would bring nearly fifty thousand dollars in all.

Tod took a deep interest in the herd, for he had roped and branded many of the calves himself. "Soon as football's over," he told his father, "I'd like to help you ship 'em."

*　　*　　*

The squad got a briefing on Monday. Dutch Kleinschmidt made no mention of the Rowell game beyond saying he hoped they had learned something. Most of his talk dealt with the upcoming game that would be played at Lundy.

"They've got a bigger school than ours," he said, "and a bigger football squad. Most of the time they use one team when they've got the ball and another when they're on defense. That defensive team, I'm told, is mighty tough to score on. It's true the Longhorns have lost two games, but one was a three-to-nothing squeaker, and in the other Skipton just nosed them out, seven to six. Their line is big and heavy, and their backs are fast. I'm not sure you can beat 'em, but I know one thing—you'll make a real try at it.

"Now," he went on, "I'm going to give you a new play—a double reverse. It'll need a lot of practice, because it's dangerous if the hand-offs aren't perfect. So, Andy, and you, Tod, will have to work on it a lot this week. Here's the diagram."

On the blackboard he sketched the play, and they all

agreed that if it worked, it would be a ground-gainer. If it didn't, there was the possibility of a recovered fumble by their opponents.

"All right," said the coach. "No scrimmage today, but let's go out and run through it a few times."

The way they practiced the new play, the team lined up with the strong side left. On the snap Andy left his position and cut behind Flick, who had faked a hand-off to one of the other backs. Flick gave the ball to Andy as he sped toward the right wing. But as soon as the defense swung over to stop him, Tod sprinted across behind Andy and took the ball for a left end sweep.

The timing, they found, had to be exactly right or one of them was sure to muff the hand-off. It wasn't until they had tried it a dozen times that everything worked properly.

"Now," said Dutch, "you can see why you'll have to keep practicing."

Day after day that week, the team went through the maneuver, and Flick made a sound suggestion.

"Wouldn't it work better," he asked, "if we ran a straight reverse first? Andy could carry around right end an' maybe make a gain. Then they'd be expecting the same thing next time, an' it would be Tod, scootin' around to the left."

The coach agreed, and both plays were given special signal numbers. Meanwhile, in scrimmage, they polished up their regular blocking, tackling, and passing. There was no skylarking among the players that week. They worked now with a kind of fiery determination that made Tod proud to be one of them.

Lundy was a town two or three times larger than Prairie. It was situated on a spur line of the Union Pacific, nearly forty miles to the north. In order to get there well ahead of game time, the buses would have to leave before noon.

By eleven-thirty on Saturday, Tod had eaten a light lunch

at home and was waiting for Mike Hoban to come for him when the phone rang.

It was Mike. "My dad's usin' the truck," he said, "an' he won't get here much before twelve. But don't worry. I'll pick you up an' we'll drive all the way to Lundy. We'll make it easy in an hour."

So Tod sat down to wait. Twenty minutes later his father came in, slamming the kitchen door behind him. His face was dark with anger.

"Trouble!" he growled. "Rustlers got away with more'n thirty head of our best steers last night!"

He went at once to the telephone and called the sheriff. "Charlie," he said. "It's Jim Ross. You had any word of cattle rustlers lately? Well, they're around. Took thirty-two head of prime steers from my feed lot last night. That's right. Looks like two big trailer trucks musta backed right up to the fence. Yep, there are pretty good tire tracks. How soon? Half an hour? OK, I'll be lookin' for you."

He hung up and turned to his son. "Guess I won't get up to Lundy to see you play," he said. "Sorry. But this is somethin' that has to be tended to right away."

"Gosh!" said Tod, shaken by the news. "Wish I could stay here to help. You think they'll be able to trace those trucks?"

"Maybe. They're pretty good at followin' clues like tire tracks. Anyhow, don't you fret about it. Go play a good game of football!"

Tod went out to the feed lot for a look. The north end of the long, fenced enclosure was nearly a quarter of a mile from the house but only a hundred yards from a side road. The wire had been cut to drive the cattle out and into the trucks, then tied neatly back in place so that the rest of the herd couldn't escape. Huge dual tires had sunk into the ground and left deep impressions. He couldn't identify the make by the treads, but he was sure the lawmen could.

116

The distant sound of a honking horn came from the highway by the house, and he saw Mike waiting in the pickup. When he waved and yelled, his friend drove down the side road to meet him.

"What's goin' on?" Mike asked. "Fence busted?'

"Worse'n that. Rustlers got more'n thirty of our beef steers, last night. Never woke Pa or me, or the hands in the bunkhouse, an' they must be a long way off by now."

"Gee! Where d'you s'pose they took 'em? All the way to Wichita?"

"Maybe," said Tod. "But if they did, the police ought to catch 'em at a roadblock somewhere along. Pa called the sheriff soon as he found out."

They drove northward through rolling range and wheat country. Both were quiet, thinking about the theft of the cattle.

"Golly," Mike murmured. "That'd be close to seventy-five hundred dollars if they got full price. Most likely, though, they'd sell to some small packer that didn't ask questions."

There wasn't much more said, but Tod couldn't get his mind off the robbery. Perhaps it was because they were both thinking about it that they noticed the two long trailers with slatted sides. They were parked beside the highway just where it entered the town of Lundy. Beyond the trucks were cattle pens and several cattle cars standing on a railroad siding.

"Hey—hold it!" Tod exclaimed, but Mike had already put on the brakes. He pulled the pickup over to the roadside in front of the trailers. Tod jumped out and went to the fence. In the enclosure a small herd of white-faced steers stood uneasily. And two men were pulling a ramp into place, leading from the chute up to the open door of a cattle car.

Tod had good eyes. He gripped the fence and stared at the nearest steer till it turned and gave him a view of its left flank.

"By thunder!" he whispered. "That's our brand!"

Mike had hurried to join him. "Sure does look like a JR," he answered. "You ought to know. But what'll we do now?"

"Stop 'em!" Tod growled. "I'll go in. You get to a phone an' call the police!"

"Not alone you don't go in—those guys'll play rough! Maybe we can handle 'em if we're together."

Without waiting, Mike climbed the fence, and Tod landed on the other side right with him. They went closer to the cattle.

"Look!" said Tod. He pointed to the clear brand mark on one of the steers. It was a monogram, with the stem of the "J" forming the vertical line of the "R."

"Hey, you!" one of the two men yelled. "Get out o'
here, kids! You want to spook the cattle?"

He left the ramp and advanced on them—a big man
with an ugly face and a paunch that hung out over his pants.

"These your steers?" asked Tod quietly.

"Don't ask fool questions. See the brand? Stands for Jenkins Ranch. That's me—Bill Jenkins. Now git—'fore I bust
you one!"

He made a threatening move toward Tod, and at that
instant Mike launched his two hundred pounds at the fat
man's midriff. He hit him with a football block that knocked
his wind out and sent him sprawling on his back.

There was the loud report of a gun. The other man,
smaller and more wiry, was running toward them, a big
Colt automatic smoking in his hand.

"Get out of here, punks!" he shouted. "An' quick, or I'll
fill you full of lead!"

He leveled the wicked-looking Colt at Mike's chest, but

the big tackle faced him steadily. Tod stood a step or two
to his left. He was scared—more for Mike than for himself—but he wasn't going to turn tail. He counted three,
then made a lightning lunge. His left hand caught the rus-
tler's arm, knocking it upward as the automatic roared
again, and in the same second he crossed his right fist hard
to the man's jaw. As the fellow staggered backward, the pistol flew out of his grasp. Mike picked it up almost before it
hit the ground.

At that moment they became aware of a newcomer. He
was an older man, with grizzled hair and hard eyes, and
there was a badge pinned to his shirt.

"All right," he said in a raspy voice. "What's goin' on
here?"

13

Tod looked the man over and decided he was all right. "These are my father's cattle," he told him bluntly. "They were rustled off our place last night."

"What's your name?"

"Tod Ross. My pa's Jim Ross. We live down near Prairie."

The man examined the brands on one or two of the steers. Then he took the gun that Mike handed him.

"I work for the Union Pacific—railroad detective," he told them. "Who was it done the shootin'?"

Tod indicated the smaller man, now on his feet.

"Don't you believe it," snarled the big one with the potbelly, who had gotten his wind back. "It was these here punks!"

"Oh? How come they had to knock you both down if they had the gun? As a matter of fact, I just got word to be on the lookout for these missin' steers. The brand's right, an' I reckon they'll be able to identify those trucks of yours by the tire tracks. Those cattle would ha' been on their way right now if the cars had been on the sidin' at five o'clock, as they were supposed to be. All four of you'd better come along to the depot, an' I'll call the sheriff's office from there."

"Hope you don't have to keep us too long," Mike put in. "Tod an' I are on the Prairie football team, an' the game starts pretty quick."

The detective nodded. "Come on, you," he told the cattle thieves. "Walk in front of me, an' don't make any funny moves."

With that he marched them down the track to the little frame depot. He had the station agent keep them covered with the pistol while he dialed the sheriff.

"He's comin' right out here," he told the boys. "Soon's you've answered a couple o' questions, I reckon he'll let you go play football."

They stood there for perhaps ten minutes, with little to do but look around at the dingy waiting room, the fly-specked travel posters, and the wire cage where the agent fumbled with his car lists and train reports. The two captives were sullen and moody, but they didn't try to escape. The old railroad dick held the big black gun on them with a steady hand.

At last the sheriff's car arrived with its siren shrieking. Followed by a deputy, he came in and took statements from Tod and Mike. Also he promised to call Tod's father at once. Then, without more ado, he snapped handcuffs on the culprits and hustled them out to the car, taking the pistol with him as evidence.

It was one-thirty by the station clock. The two boys thanked the gray-haired detective and departed. In the pickup they drove through town as fast as the law allowed and reached the high school just as the other members of the team were coming out of the gym in their uniforms. There was no time for explanations. They took Kleinschmidt's reproachful look without a word and rushed inside to suit up.

There was plenty of excitement on the field when they ran out a few minutes later. Both bands were playing, and

122

the Lundy stands were packed to capacity. A surprising number of Prairie supporters were on hand, too, and the cheerleaders were whooping it up. Winning this game meant a lot to both communities.

The two boys rushed into the warm-up formation immediately, and it wasn't until several minutes later, when the captains were called on the field, that Tod had a chance to look over the Longhorn squad. They wore black-and-gold jerseys that made them look even bigger than they really were, and that was formidable enough. There were a lot of them, too—thirty or forty players in all.

Flick won the toss and elected to receive. There was only a light breeze blowing, but Lundy took advantage of it in choosing the west end of the field. The kickoff was a good one, long and straight down the middle. Instead of trying to catch it on the five, Andy Willis let it roll across the goal line, and it was brought out to the twenty.

On the first play, Flick tested out the big defensive line. Weil was stopped for a two-yard gain at center. Then a cross buck, with Joe Luke carrying, gained only another yard. Still playing conservative football, Flick hit the line once more for short yardage, then called for a punt. Weil's kick was high enough to let the ends get down under it, and Tod tackled the ballcarrier on the enemy's forty-two.

With good field position, the Longhorn quarterback threw a short pass over the line that reached the fifty. Then, in two ground plays, Lundy got its first down and was a few yards into Prairie territory.

"Drive in there hard an' hold 'em," Flick urged in the huddle. "We want to make 'em open up with some passes."

The line charged low and hard, and the Longhorn tailback was stopped cold. As Flick had predicted, the Lundy quarter now decided to go to the air, and the Cowboys were ready. Mike tore through a hole between guard and tackle and crashed the pocket, hurrying the quarterback's throw.

Instead of the long pass he had intended, it came wobbling over toward Tod's side of the line. The left end scrambled back, reaching for the ball, but Tod jumped a second quicker and a few inches higher. His big, sure hands took it in midair, and before the disgruntled end could tackle him, he was running diagonally toward the sideline. He cut past two pursuers and was finally brought down by the safety man, only a dozen yards from pay dirt.

Flick's motto was, "Hit 'em while they're groggy!" He called the huddle together while the defensive team was straggling on the field and gave his men the play.

It was a double fake, first to Joe Luke, then to Weil, the tailback. And finally, dropping back, Flick tossed a pass to Andy. It was perfectly timed, beautifully thrown, and the little end took it just before it hit the ground. He was across the goal line when he caught it. A big back slammed into him viciously, but he hung on, and a wild cheer rose from the Prairie rooters. A moment later it turned to a groan, for Andy lay there very still, obviously injured.

After he was carried off the field, the angry Cowboys kicked the extra point, and the score was seven to nothing.

When they lined up to kick off, Rudy Ryker was put in at Tod's position, and Tod was shifted to left end. He had never played on that side of the line, but it didn't make too much difference as long as they were on defense.

The first play from scrimmage was an end sweep aimed his way. He saw it coming, fooled the lead blocker with a feint to the left, and dodged past in time to nail the ball-carrier for no gain. After that they avoided his end. Con-centrating on line plays, the Longhorns hammered out one first down, then another, and were almost to midfield.

There the Prairie defense stiffened, and on third down with six yards to go, the Lundy quarterback tried a pass. All the Cowboys were ready. Three backs opened out to cover the receivers, Weil and Carey crouched behind the line, waiting to shoot the gap, and Tod edged in, closer to the tackle. When the passer dropped back, all three of them crashed through to swarm him under before he could get rid of the ball.

With fourth down and more than fifteen to go, the Longhorns had nothing to do but punt. It was a poor kick, and Flick, now playing deep, took it on his own thirty. With good blocks from Joe Luke and Mike Hoban, he zigzagged forward to the forty-seven. There he called the team into the huddle.

"Can't use that double reverse play without Andy," he said, "but we can try the end around. How about it, Tod?"

"Sure," he answered, and the rest agreed. Flick faked his hand-offs to the charging backs while Tod raced across behind the line. He took the short backward pass from the quarterback, cut inside the opposing end, and barreled through for a first down in Longhorn territory.

"Good!" Flick told the team. "There's a Skipton scout in the stands, an' I wanted to be sure he got a good look at that play. Come on—let's hit the line now!"

Two plunges off tackle netted only five yards, and as they lined up again, Tod could see the defenders back-pedaling, sure that a pass was coming. He grinned to himself, and on the snap he sped downfield, watching over his shoulder. But as he knew, Flick had no intention of passing. Instead, the quarterback faked a throw, tucked the ball under his arm, and darted to his right. With a clear path ahead, he sprinted all the way to the twenty on a perfectly executed keeper play.

Backed up against their goal line now, the big Lundy forwards dug in grimly to stop the assault. The first play into the line gained only a yard, and an end sweep added three more. The ball was on the sixteen now, midway be-

tween the sidelines. There Flick called for a short flare pass
to Tod, but he was blitzed as he threw, and the pass went
incomplete.

"All right, Aaron," he told the fullback with a grin.
"Guess it's up to you to kick one. Hold 'em, you linemen,
an' give him a chance."

He knelt to take the pass from center, and Weil, cool and
steady, put the ball over the bar.

The score was ten to nothing in Prairie's favor, and it
stayed that way for most of the first half. Then, with only
a minute to play, the Longhorns' two-hundred-pound fullback went over from the two-yard line, and they kicked the
extra point. When they went into the gym, the Cowboys'
lead was only three points—ten to seven.

Everybody was anxious about Andy. He sat there grin-
ning, his torso taped up with bandages, and told them the
doctor said he had a couple of broken ribs.

"He thinks I'm through playin' for the season," Andy
said. "But I aim to fool him. Long as I keep strapped up
tight, I reckon I can still run!"

Dutch Kleinschmidt laughed. "You're a game chicken,
Andy," he said, "but the doctor's right. We've got to learn
to get along without you, so you'll be in shape to play next
year."

After that the coach talked to the team while they rested.
Hanging onto that slim lead wouldn't be easy, he told them.
With their two-platoon system, the Longhorns would have
an edge as the second half wore on.

"What I hope you'll do is score again while you're fresh,"
he said. "Then just hold on the best you can."

He took Flick Davis aside to discuss strategy, and at that
moment the door of the dressing room was flung open. The
man who came bursting in was none other than big Jim
Ross.

126

"Where's that boy of mine?" he roared. "An' where's Mike Hoban?"

Then his craggy face broke into a grin. "Maybe you fellers don't know it," he said, "but these two pretty near missed the game. They were busy catchin' cattle rustlers over here at the Union Pacific yards. What's the score?"

Tod told him it was ten to seven in the Cowboys' favor. "But," he added, "we had some tough luck. Andy's hurt."

"He's right," said Kleinschmidt. "And you all know what that means. The rest of you'll have to play twice as hard."

Prairie would be kicking off, and the coach left Tod in at left end, with Rudy Ryker in his former position. The kick was long, and the safety man let it roll over the line. The Longhorns started from the twenty, hit quickly for a first down, then ran into trouble. A line play made only a yard or two. The quarterback was blitzed, back on the twenty-two, and on third down, with long yardage, he elected to punt.

It was a good kick, and Flick had to take it on the bounce, back on the thirty. Two tacklers downed him there in his tracks.

"Guess your old man was sort o' happy about those steers," Mike told Tod as they left the huddle.

"Yep," Tod replied. "But he won't be happy if we don't win."

Two plays into the line worked the ball out to the thirty-seven, and Flick called the signal for a flare pass to Tod. He edged out, darted past the opposing end, and caught the ball on the forty-one, where he was tackled at the sideline. The Longhorn captain insisted on a measurement, but it was a first down by half a yard. During the brief time-out, Dutch called Ryker out of the lineup, sent Tod to his usual post at right end, and sent in Cal Reagan from the scrubs to play on the left wing. Reagan was only fifteen, a sophomore, but he was rangy and eager and liked to play football.

As they lined up, Flick nodded to Tod, and he sauntered out to the lonesome end post.

The Lundy defense spotted him. A linebacker and two deep backs hurried over to cover the expected pass. They left young Reagan practically free, and before the defenders could get back again, he had caught a beautifully aimed floater. He reached the Lundy forty-five before he was brought down.

"Nice catch, kid! Good goin', Cal!" the first-stringers told him in the huddle. And Flick grinned.

"Now they know we've got two ends that can take passes," he said. "Reckon they'll be a little confused."

Now that they had a first down in enemy territory, he called one ground play, then sent both ends out wide. A fake hand-off to Weil gave Joe Luke time to get into the flat beyond the Longhorn line. There he caught a bullet jump pass and ran it all the way to the thirty.

"Time to hit 'em with the bomb," said Flick. "Get down as fast as you can, Tod. An' you linemen an' backs, give me some protection! I can't throw till he's in position."

On the snap Tod was away, sprinting at top speed. He was already at the goal line when he looked back and found himself surrounded by three big Longhorns. The ball, he saw, was coming far to his left. He faked a stride straight ahead, twisted past the defensive back, and leaped with all his strength. His fingers touched the ball, deflected it over the safety man's head, then with a full-length dive he caught it before it hit the ground.

As he got to his feet, clutching the football, he was nearly deafened by the yells from the Cowboy stand. And right beside him he saw the referee holding both hands aloft to signal a touchdown.

128

A moment later Weil had kicked the extra point, and their lead was seventeen to seven. But now the Longhorn offensive team would have the ball, and they were big and fresh. Coach Kleinschmidt gave Reagan a rest and added weight to the line by putting Rudy back in at left end.

Tod was looking forward to a hard grind if they were to hold the Longhorns the rest of the way. But almost at once they got a break. Aaron Weil arched his kick high, to give the tacklers more time to get downfield. Hemmed in by Cowboys, the safety man should have called for a fair catch. Instead, he wanted to run with the ball, and Mike Hoban's jarring tackle knocked it out of his arms. Tod was right there. He grabbed the ball in the air and ran straight ahead across the goal line. Once more Aaron's toe made the point after touchdown, and the Cowboys were ahead by a twenty-four to seven score.

Battle as they would, the Longhorns couldn't overcome that lead. Before the end of the final quarter they got close enough to kick a field goal, but as the game ended, they were beaten, twenty-four to ten.

14

As Tod plodded toward the dressing room, the bus that had brought the Cowboy band and cheerleaders was loading for the trip home. Mary Ann Foster caught sight of him and ran over, her face aglow with the light of victory.

"Great game, Tod!" she cried. "You were terrific! Listen —this next week is the 4-H Fair, and they'll be judging calves on Thursday night. Can you come? I want you to see Buttercup take a ribbon!"

"Sure," he told her. "I guess I can make it. What time?"

"They usually start around seven. Why don't you come for dinner and drive over with us?"

He hesitated, not wanting to seem too eager. Then he accepted. "I'll be there," he said. "Thanks."

After his shower he found his father waiting for him. "You know that pair of cattle thieves you an' Mike caught?" he said. "They're wanted in Texas an' Oklahoma for the same thing. Sheriff's got flyers on 'em, an' the Cattlemen's Association's offered a reward. Guess what you two boys'll get. Five thousand dollars! Soon as they're convicted, you'll have twenty-five hundred apiece!"

Tod was speechless, staring at his father.

"Of course," Jim Ross added, "we may have to testify

at the trial, but I reckon it'll be pretty cut an' dried. Come on—get dressed. I'll take you home."

During the ride Tod found his tongue and told his father the story of the capture. "The funny thing," he said, "was that we were both thinking about those rustlers when, all of a sudden, we saw the two trailer trucks. Then I got a look at the steers an' was certain. The fight didn't amount to much. Mike knocked the big guy kicking, an' when the other one was going to shoot him, I grabbed his gun arm. But you know if we'd been five minutes later, those cattle woulda been in the cars. How's that for luck!"

He had to give the details again, first to the two hired hands, then to Mrs. McDonald. She was late with supper, having been talking to friends on the telephone most of the afternoon. The tale of the rustlers and their capture had spread through the area like wildfire. And it seemed to have put the victory over Lundy completely in the shade.

"I reckon it's time to ship the steers to market," Jim Ross remarked as he ate. "They're about heavy enough, an' I'd like to get 'em off my hands before somebody else tries to steal 'em. I'll order the trucks for Monday."

"Well," said Tod, "I guess you won't need me." He remembered the days when he was a small boy and the herd was driven to the yards in Prairie on foot. That was more exciting, but also harder on the stock. Now there were police regulations against cattle drives on the highway, so they had to travel by truck.

The Sunday paper rather belittled Prairie's win over Lundy. "Nobody expected the Longhorns to do much," the sportswriter observed, "since they lost a lot of lettermen and have a green team. The fact that they held Prairie so well in the first half is a credit to good coaching. And by next season, those big youngsters should make a real run at the Tri-County crown. In spite of getting several breaks, the Cowboys had one piece of hard luck. They lost their

132

star end and runback artist, little Andy Willis, who is out with several broken ribs. The injury may cost Prairie any slight chance they had for the championship.

"Skipton proved again that it's the class of the league. The Skeeters handed Logansville an artistic lacing, and the final score was 33-7. Skipton has the speed and deception that should clinch the crown next Saturday when they invade the stronghold of the Prairie Cowboys. Both teams now have six and one records."

"Hunh!" growled Tod's father. "I knew that guy was prejudiced! Don't say a word about you—or Flick Davis— or any of the rest. What about Andy, anyhow? Any chance he can play?"

"Not much, I'm afraid. We're sure going to miss him if he's out o' the game."

* * *

The news at school that Monday was far from encouraging. Andy had gone to the hospital for X-rays, and it was reported that the ribs were cracked rather than broken. However, the doctor had forbidden him to take any part in the practice for a full week. He came ambling into the briefing session that afternoon, a sheepish grin on his face.

The team rose as one man and cheered him. But when he tried to thank them, they could tell that every breath hurt.

"Strapped up so tight," he said, "I can't even laugh. But you guys don't need me to win. You did all right Saturday, after I was out."

Coach Kleinschmidt shook his head. "We'll sure miss you, Andy," he said. "But we'll just have to work a lot harder to make up for it."

He turned to the rest of the squad. "These Skipton Skeeters," he told them, "are probably faster than any team we've met. They won't outweigh us, but they can move that ball. Two of their backs have run the hundred in ten flat. Then they've got a tall, rangy end who plays center on the basketball team. He catches most of their passes. And finally, their quarterback can throw almost as well as Flick.

"To beat them, we've got to fight for every yard. And we've got to come up with a new play or two. They've scouted us and know about what we'll do in any given situation. At least, they *think* they know. We may be able to fool 'em. One thing I'd like to try is to have Tod do a bit of passing."

He went to the blackboard and sketched the play. It would start as an end around, with Tod taking the hand-off from Flick. Then, when the defense came in to stop him, he would throw a pass—to the left end or one of the backs.

"Tod," he said, "I'd like you and Cal Reagan to go out right now and practice passing and catching. Tomorrow we'll try it in scrimmage."

Tod had no idea whether his passes would be any good, but he was always willing to try. After half an hour he found he was getting better direction on the ball and delivering it faster. He also practiced throwing on the run, for the new trick play would probably call for a running pass. To his delight young Cal Reagan proved he had a lot of natural ability. He wasn't as tall as Tod, and his hands were smaller, but he rarely juggled or dropped the ball. Best of all, the boy was eager to make good. Until Andy's injury, playing on the first team had been beyond his wildest hopes. Now the chance was his, and he wasn't going to miss it.

After a while Dutch and Flick came out to watch from the sideline. Both seemed to like what they saw, and the quarterback congratulated Tod when it was over.

"I can give you a couple o' pointers," he said, "like how to lead the receiver a little more. But I never threw the ball

134

on the run as well as you do. I bet this play's goin' to work fine!"

Tod was pleased, but he wanted Reagan to share some of the praise. "Don't forget," he said, "it's this kid here that's making me look good. He's a natural!"

Dutch Kleinschmidt nodded. "He'll fit in all right," he replied. "OK, boys, you can go ahead home."

Mike brought the pickup around, and Tod got in. "Town's beginnin' to get excited about this game," said the big tackle with a grin. "I reckon there won't be any empty seats, come Saturday."

As they drove down Main Street, there was plenty of evidence to back Mike's statement. Half the stores had big posters in their windows. They were hand-lettered but effective. BEAT SKIPTON! they urged. SLAP THE SKEETERS DOWN! TRI-COUNTY CHAMPS—PRAIRIE COWBOYS!

Somebody had been hard at work, and Tod had a hunch that somebody was Mary Ann. On Tuesday he found he was right.

"What do you think of our campaign, Tod?" she asked him as they went into history class. "I've practically had to get down on my knees to some of our leading merchants to get those posters up. But I think they're beginning to feel some public spirit at last!"

Tod laughed. "Even old Mr. Watkins, at the First National Bank?" he asked. "I thought I saw a small poster there, too."

"You did. After all, I guess my dad's their biggest depositor, so why wouldn't he be nice to me?"

There was nothing boastful about the remark. Mary Ann was merely stating a fact of life, and if she had used her name to convince Mr. Watkins, why, more power to her!

"We're going to hold another pep rally Friday night," she continued, "and we want to have the whole squad there. If it's decent weather, we should get half the town out to the rally. And, Tod—don't forget our date Thursday evening!"

Tod wasn't likely to forget. He had been thinking about going to dinner at the Fosters' with a mixture of pleasure and dread. He hoped his table manners would pass muster and wondered if he should dress up. Even the word "dinner" had an ominous sound. On the ranch the evening meal was just plain supper.

On Tuesday there was a stiff practice, with Tod and Cal Reagan at the ends. When the scrubs had the ball, Rudy Ryker replaced Cal for defensive purposes, and Cal moved over to the second team. He continued to show real ability at catching passes, and he could move fast once he had the ball. The coach didn't let the youngster work too long, however.

"He's our ace in the hole with Andy out," he explained to Tod and Flick. "Don't want him to get hurt or used up before the game."

The air was unusually warm that week—more like August than November. Farmers and ranchers listened anxiously to the radio forecasts, for, as Jim Ross remarked, it felt like a "weather-breeder."

"Pretty late in the season for a cyclone," he admitted. "But there's a cold front movin' into the mountains out o' Canada, an' snow's started already in Montana. If that front comes down this way an' tangles with the heat wave, we'd better watch out."

Tod had never felt the force of a real tornado, but once, when he was ten, his father had taken him over to Logansville to see the aftermath of one, and he wasn't likely to forget it. The wind funnel had cut a path only a hundred yards wide that leveled every house and tree for two miles. Most homes had cyclone cellars where the family holed up when a big wind was coming. And so, despite the fearful damage, the loss of life hadn't been high.

136

On Wednesday the temperature rose to the low nineties, and the boys sweltered through their practice with little enthusiasm. A sultry south wind brought humidity up from the Gulf, but meanwhile the cold front had advanced into Wyoming.

"What you want to do, Pa?" Tod asked that night. "Think we should get the stock up to the corral?"

"Nope. They're better off out on the range, where they can scatter. I hope that school o' yours has some kind of underground shelter, though."

"Gee—you really think we might get a cyclone?"

"Can't tell. About all anybody can do is keep tuned in to the radio an' hope if there's a twister it goes somewhere else."

The pupils at Prairie High School were edgy on Thursday morning. The hot wind blew harder, wailing around the corners of the building and sifting dust in at the windows.

At two o'clock that afternoon, word went out from the principal's office that school would close early. The buses wheeled up to the main door. After some debate, Coach Kleinschmidt decided to cancel football practice, and Tod got into Mike's pickup for the ride home.

Just as they started, he caught sight of Mary Ann. "Hey!" he called. "Is the 4-H Fair still on?"

She ran nearer, the wind whipping at her hair. "That's what they say," she shouted. "Anyhow, I'll see you around six."

Mike grinned at him as he let in the clutch. "You steppin' out in society?" he asked. "Good boy! Sounds like you're makin' progress!"

* * *

Tod put on a clean white shirt, tucked it into his tight stockman's pants, and adjusted his string tie with care. The good Texas boots would pass, he thought, and he had a gabardine jacket without too much embroidery on it. The general effect, seen in the mirror, wasn't bad, he decided.

He had mentioned his date to his father, and Jim Ross made no objection. "Just go careful," he told the boy. "Not likely we'll have a cyclone after sundown, but keep an eye on the weather."

Tod saddled the buckskin pony and swung himself up. Buck's eyes rolled, and he snorted at the hot feel of the wind. Then, as they moved out toward the road, a sudden clap of thunder made the horse jump.

"Steady, now, boy," Tod told him soothingly. More thunder followed, and there were vivid snakes of lightning in the southern sky. Tod wondered if he had time to go back and get a slicker, then decided against it. The clouds were black enough, but so far no rain had fallen.

He urged the pony into a gallop and rode on along the dirt shoulder of the highway. At six o'clock he entered the Foster gate and hitched Buck to the porch rail.

Mary Ann must have been watching, for almost at once she flung open the front door.

"Is it raining yet?" she called cheerfully. "You're right on time, but I was afraid you'd get wet."

She ushered Tod in, and again there stood Wade Foster, ready to greet him. This time the big man wore a business suit, and behind him Tod saw a pretty woman with snapping dark eyes like her daughter's.

"Mother," said Mary Ann, "this is our star right end, Tod Ross. Tod, you've already met my dad."

Tod shook hands with them both in bashful silence. Then Mrs. Foster urged them to come into the dining room.

"It does look like rain," she said, "and I think we should have dinner and get out to the judging before we're all drenched. So let's sit down at once."

Awkwardly Tod held Mrs. Foster's chair for her, then

138

sat down at her right, opposite Mary Ann. A young maid in a white cap and apron waited on them, and the food was delicious. After the first stiffness had worn off, Tod felt more at ease.

He was just starting to answer Wade Foster's questions about the football team when a violent thunderclap shook the house and the lights went out.

15

"Don't worry now, girls," said Mr. Foster calmly. "It probably hit a transformer somewhere down the line. Current should come on again pretty soon. Here, I'll light some candles, and, Mary Ann, have you got that transistor radio handy? Maybe we can pick up a weather report."

Mary Ann nodded in the flickering candlelight. "I'll get it right away. But I think Tod should put his horse under cover before it rains hard. Here's a flashlight."

Tod took the light and went out at once. The air now felt heavy and lifeless, and the sky, not yet fully dark, had a queer greenish look. With Buck safely tied in the barn, Tod hurried back to the house.

The electricity was still off, but the Fosters sat at the table once more. The frightened maid cleared away the dishes and brought in the dessert.

"I hope you'll like that apple pie, Tod," said Mary Ann. "I made it myself."

She fiddled with the controls of the little radio, and finally it produced some sounds. Through the static they could hear a man's voice announcing some kind of news bulletin.

". . . seems to be following . . . river valley . . . track-

140

ing north from the Oklahoma line . . . several houses in Wykoff . . . roof off . . . no deaths reported."

"That's a tornado warning!" said Wade Foster. "Heading this way, too. I reckon the power-line poles are down, an' that's why we lost our lights."

"Oh!" cried Mary Ann. "Poor little Buttercup! She's all alone in that strange place. Daddy, can't we go over there right now?"

Foster, as Tod could see, hated to deny his daughter anything. He debated the question nearly a minute before he answered. "All right," he said at last. "I think we'll be safe in the car. I'll take you and Tod. Ruth, you'd better take Lulu and go right down to the cyclone cellar. Here's a flashlight. You'll find candles down there."

He kissed his wife, and she obeyed him at once. Then the three who were left went out to the garage. As the big Cadillac purred into motion, Tod felt a tingling in his skin. The lights bored through the dark, and suddenly the wind came in howling gusts. It was rapidly growing colder, too.

"That's the front coming through," said Foster tersely.

It was only two miles to the fairgrounds, and there was almost no traffic on the road. As they pulled up by the big pavilion, they could see a few lights inside and hear the chugging of a Diesel engine. An emergency generator had been started up.

Only a handful of people were around the pavilion, and most of them were anxious 4-H Club members. The animals to be shown were still in the stable tents that ringed the main structure.

"Buttercup's in Tent B," Mary Ann shouted above the shriek of the wind. "Over this way!"

She ran the fifty yards to the tent, with Tod close behind her. Wade Foster followed at a walk. A single swaying electric bulb hung from its cord inside, and by its dim light

Mary Ann hurried to one pen in the line that ran down the middle of the tent. Tod could see other calves—stocky Herefords and Angus, big black-and-white Holsteins. There seemed to be only a couple of Guernseys in the group.

Little Buttercup was huddled in a corner of her pen, her big deer-eyes wide with fright.

"You poor baby!" Mary Ann exclaimed, and cuddled the calf's body against her. And just then her father shouted from the tent door.

"Here it comes!" he bellowed. "Lie down—flat on the ground!"

Tod pulled the unwilling girl down beside him. A tremendous roar filled his ears. It was like the thunder of a dozen express trains. The sound mounted in fury, then passed on, and Tod scrambled to his feet. As he did so, there was another sound—a terrible metallic crash—and a distant scream that they knew came from a human throat.

They looked about them, half stunned. The tent shook violently, but its canvas was still there. By the door Wade Foster stared out.

"Great grief!" he muttered. "Look at that!"

The sheet-metal roof of the pavilion was gone, Tod saw, though its concrete walls still stood. Beyond, where other tents had been, there was only a pile of tattered canvas. The twister had cut a path through the middle of the fairgrounds, hardly more than the width of a football field, Tod thought. But everything in that path was torn or twisted or blown away.

"Come on!" he called. "I heard a yell. Somebody's hurt!"

Without waiting for the older man, he raced across to the ruined pavilion. A light bulb, miraculously still working, showed chairs and part of the judging ring piled in wild confusion against the north wall. From the splintered mass there came once more a cry for help, weaker this time.

Tod began tearing at the wreckage with frenzied hands. In a moment Wade Foster joined him, and they tossed the wooden chairs behind them as they bored into the pile.

"Where are you?" Tod called. "Holler again so we can find you!"

"Here!" cried the voice, almost directly in front of where he had been digging. It was only a minute or two more before the rescuers caught sight of the victim's legs. Frantically they jerked away more debris and pulled out a teenage boy.

"Cal Reagan!" Tod panted. "Are you all right?"

"My arm feels like it's busted," the youngster said through gritted teeth. "Guess I'm lucky, though. I'm alive! I was the only one in here."

Foster felt the boy's left arm. "It's broken, all right," he told Tod. "Help me get him in the car, and I'll take him to the doctor. You stay here and look after Mary Ann."

When the Cadillac had gone, Tod ran back to the tent.

"Buttercup's over her scare," said Mary Ann. "Look—she's eating some hay. What did you find over there?"

"Bad news," he told her. "Things are in quite a mess at the pavilion. Young Cal Reagan was setting up chairs when the roof blew off. He got his arm broken, but we dug him out, an' your father's taken him to the doctor. Come on—we ought to go look for more hurt folks!"

Fortunately Mary Ann still had her flashlight. They ran together toward the area north of the pavilion, where the tornado had passed. Most of the ground was swept bare, but they soon came to a heap of ragged, dripping canvas.

"Anybody here?" called Tod.

The answer was a pitiful bleating sound. "The lambs!" Mary Ann exclaimed. "They must have been in this tent—poor things!"

Pulling away the sodden cloth was a job that took all the power of their strong young arms. But the plaintive bleating continued and led them at last to the trapped animals. There were two lambs in one pen, both alive and unhurt. Only yards away they found the bodies of two more that had been killed.

By that time cars were streaming into the fairgrounds, and there were plenty of men to take over the grim search. The huge sheet-metal roof had landed a quarter of a mile away in an open field, but in its flight it had cut through two power poles and taken the top off a tree. By the luckiest of chances, only some of the livestock had been killed, and the single human casualty was Cal Reagan.

"Poor guy!" said Tod, thinking of the young end. "He was sure keen to play against Skipton. An' he was a real help to the team, too."

"I know," Mary Ann told him. "I watched you throwing passes to him. It's a shame. But I'm glad the tornado came tonight and not tomorrow. I hate to think what might have happened to our rally!"

When Wade Foster returned with the Cadillac, his daughter insisted on loading her calf into the back seat. Clean straw was piled on the rich upholstery, and the two young people carried the little Guernsey to the car. The 4-H judging would have to be postponed for a week or more.

They got the calf back into her comfortable stall in the Foster barn, and Tod tried to call his father. The telephone wires were dead, so feeling that Jim Ross might be worried about him, he said good night to his hostess and rode back home.

It was a comfort to see all the ranch buildings standing black against the sky. No damage had been done except that the power was still off. And as soon as he entered the kitchen, he saw his father reading the paper by candlelight.

"Well, how'd it go, Tod?" he asked casually. "The Foster girl win any ribbons?"

144

"Gosh, Pa!" said Tod. "You mean you didn't hear about the twister?"

"Twister? Nope. Radio's off, along with the lights. What happened?"

Tod described the tornado and what it had done to the pavilion and tents. "When I came away," he concluded, "they hadn't found any people's bodies. But losing young Cal Reagan's sure going to be hard on the Cowboys."

The temperature dropped that night, and though the rough north wind had abated, there was ice on the puddles when Tod rose Friday morning. He did his chores, wrapped up against the chill, and when he came in, Mrs. McDonald announced that the electric power had been restored.

"A good thing, too," she said, "or you wouldn'ta had any breakfast."

Tod rode to school as usual with Mike Hoban, and once more he had to give an account of the tornado. The radio had carried the news that the twister had been a small one, as such things went. Only eighteen homes were damaged and a dozen people hurt. There were no deaths. The pavilion at the fairgrounds would be restored as quickly as possible.

Tod saw Mary Ann for a minute on the way to class. "The rally's still on for tonight," she said. "I hope you'll come. Flick's promised to be there, and Mike, and the coach."

"Sure," he told her. "I'll try."

There was serious business to take up at the squad's briefing session that afternoon. Cal's broken arm seemed to have made their special trick play impossible, and Dutch told them they'd have to concentrate on straight football, with an occasional pass to Tod or one of the backs.

"Can't even count on working the lonesome end stunt," he added. "I know for a fact that Skipton's had scouts watching the last two or three games."

Andy Willis was there, cheerful as ever, except when he moved too quickly and caused a twinge in his cracked ribs. Then they could see him wince. "Sure wish I could be in there with you guys!" he said wistfully. "Doc says I can get dressed an' sit on the bench, anyhow."

"Well, boys," the coach told them finally, "that's all for today. Get a good night's sleep. First, though, I hope as many of you as can make it will be at the rally. The kids have done a lot o' work on it, and we want 'em to know we appreciate their support."

On the way home Mike told Tod he would pick him up at seven, so they could get back to town before the rally started.

*   *   *

Close to a thousand Prairie citizens of all ages were gathered beside the bonfire that night. And there were other rooters for the team who had driven in from miles around.

The Cowboy squad was cheered individually and collectively, while the girl cheerleaders whooped it up and turned cartwheels. Then various players were called on for speeches. Tod did his best to get out of it, but Mike and Mary Ann dragged him up on the stand.

"I don't feel as if I rightly belong up here," he told the crowd, "because I've only played this one season. I can tell you, though, I'm mighty proud to be on this team. It's true we've had some bad breaks. But I know every one of us will do his darndest to win tomorrow."

With that he jumped down, while the yells of the fans rang loudly in his ears.

After the varsity players had had their say, Dutch Kleinschmidt wound it up with a short, earnest speech of thanks to the loyal rooters.

"Some of you may have heard already," he said, "that if we can bring the championship here to Prairie, the Chamber

146

of Commerce promises to raise the money for new uniforms next year. Of course that gives us an added incentive to win —if we needed one! The boys have done pretty well in their old rags, but they'll be mighty proud to step out in something better. So we aim to beat Skipton—and hold the C. of C. men to their pledge!"

"Hey—how 'bout that!" Mike murmured in Tod's ear. "Looks like we've plain got to win now!"

"Yep," said Tod. "But we knew that without the new suits."

They drove home through a cold, clear night that promised good football weather. Jim Ross was still up when Tod entered the ranch house.

"Hey, Pa," he called. "Did you hear what the Prairie Chamber o' Commerce is going to do?"

"Yep. Matter of fact, I suggested it to 'em. We figured the school board would never have enough money for new equipment, so it was up to the town's businessmen."

"Gee, Pa!" Tod exlaimed. "I won't tell anybody it was your idea, but I'm sure proud of you."

As he expected, his father grunted and looked uncomfortable. "Don't forget," he growled. "You've got to earn those suits first."

It was Tod's turn to be serious. "We aim to beat 'em if we can," he said. "But if we don't, it won't be for lack o' trying. Good night, now. I've got to get to bed."

Almost before he knew it, it was Saturday morning and the sun was shining in his eyes. For a moment he couldn't think why this was a special day. Then in a flash he remembered. It was the day of the great game—the final game of the season—the game for the championship!

16

Since he didn't plan to eat any lunch, Tod enjoyed a good, big breakfast, and Mrs. McDonald was happy to watch the food disappear.

"I hear they've started puttin' a new roof on that pavilion over at the fairgrounds," she remarked. "The one that got blowed off in the tornado. Aim to have it ready for the 4-H kids by next week."

"That's good," Tod told her. "What else is new?" He was well aware that the housekeeper was a famous gossip, and it was obvious she had something else on her mind.

"Well," she said, "I've got a friend, Mary Dennis, over Skipton way. She says their team's comin' over loaded for bear. Offered to bet me on the game. 'Course I ain't a bettin' woman, but I'd like a chance to crow over her. Tell me, now. What do you think?"

"All I can say," Tod answered, "is that we'll do our level best. We're the underdogs, an' I reckon that's the way I like it."

His father came in at that moment. "Right," he said. "You aren't so likely to get overconfident an' ease off. I aim to be there. Want to ride in with me?"

"Thanks, Pa, but Mike said he'd drop by to pick me up,

so I'd better go with him. Why don't you take Mrs. Mack? I bet she'd like to see the game."

Somewhat flustered, Mrs. McDonald finally agreed to go and hurried off to change her clothes.

Game time was one-thirty, and when Mike and Tod reached the school, an hour ahead, the stands were already beginning to fill up. A long cavalcade of cars from Skipton came down Main Street, with horns blowing and rooters yelling. From every car flew a streamer bearing the words, BEAT PRAIRIE!

"Guess they mean business," said Mike with a chuckle.

Mary Ann and her cheerleaders had been busy, too. Across the whole top of the Prairie stand ran a huge banner that said, GO, COWBOYS—GO! in letters six feet high.

In the dressing room there was no horseplay, and no one felt like kidding around. The boys were serious. Tod supposed they all felt as he did—nervous and keyed-up. He gave special attention to his equipment, making sure each strap was tight, tying his shoelaces solidly. And all the time the signals and plays were going through his head.

Dutch Kleinschmidt moved among them cheerfully, helping them get ready. When it was time to go out, he had a few words to say.

"You've all worked hard," he told them. "There isn't much more I can do for you now. From now till the game is over, it'll be up to each of you whether you turn out to be champs or runners-up. Go get 'em!"

They rose and went clumping out in their cleated shoes, their eyes blinking at the sudden sunshine. In their sober mood, it came as a surprise to hear the solid roar that went up when they appeared. Tod felt his blood begin to tingle as the squad broke into a trot. The first team lined up quickly to run through its plays, with Rudy Ryker at left end.

A short time later the captains were called out to midfield

for the toss of the coin. Tod saw the referee pat the Skipton man on the back. That meant Skipton had won the toss and would receive. And a moment later the Cowboys were taking their positions behind the forty-yard line as they prepared to kick. Opposite them the Skeeter team, resplendent in orange and green, were getting in their places to receive.

Aaron Weil's toe met the ball cleanly, sending it long and high down the middle. One of the famous Skeeter scatbacks took it on his twelve, hesitated a couple of counts, then streaked past the first tacklers. On the twenty he picked up some blockers and sped on, getting all the way to the forty-two before Flick Davis tackled him.

They lined up quickly, and their fullback hit just inside left tackle. He wasn't big, but he was fast, and the line gave him room to go through for an eight-yard gain. The obvious play would be another line plunge for a first down, but as they soon found out, Skipton rarely did what was expected. A look-in pass over center was caught for another ten yards.

"Come on, gang," Flick growled in the huddle. "They're in our territory! Let's hold 'em!"

A quickly executed sweep came around Tod's end, and he took a savage pleasure in crashing though the interference. One of his outstretched hands grabbed at the ballcarrier's ankle. He couldn't hold it, but he forced the back to stumble, and the play stopped right at the scrimmage line.

"That's the way," Flick told the team. "Now they may try anything. Just be ready to stop whatever they throw at us."

It turned out to be a flare pass to the Skeeter right end, but Rudy Ryker, playing above himself, was through in time to reach up a big arm and bat it down. With a third and ten situation, Tod was sure this would be a pass. It started out that way, with the quarter dropping back. But then, with lightning speed, he swung his foot into the ball for a quick kick. In one of the bad breaks that sometimes hit a tensed-

150

up team, Tony Fortunato's lifted hand touched the ball as it flew past. It was deflected away from the safety man, and a Skeeter end, speeding down under the kick, picked it up and ran for a touchdown.

The Cowboy rooters sat stunned by the suddenness of this development, while screams of joy rose from across the field. With the game hardly two minutes old, the visitors led by six points. And seconds later their place-kicker made it seven.

"Buck up, gang!" Flick told the team. "They've had their luck. Now let's make the breaks come our way!"

Calmly he dropped back to his own ten-yard line and prepared to take the kickoff. It was a low, hard-driven ball that came down on the thirty-five and skittered on for another ten yards. Flick picked it up and set sail, dodging behind his blockers, twisting out of tacklers' hands or changing pace to avoid them. Again and again Tod thought he was down, but the quarterback kept going. At the forty, he cut over toward the right sideline, and Tod was there to give him the key block he needed. To a hysterical roar of cheers he sprinted on, just inside the white line, crossing marker after marker. At last he was caught from behind, but not until he was on the Skipton twelve.

Tod helped him to his feet, and Flick motioned with his arms for the team to huddle quickly. Talking was more than he could manage at the moment, for his zigzag course must have covered more than a hundred yards. When he got enough breath, he gasped out the play—a buttonhook pass to Tod.

The line crouched, and the backfield men were in position. Then, on a quick count, Flick took the ball from center. Tod, plunging ahead at the snap, could only imagine the fake hand-off to Aaron Weil, then the quarterback's retreat into the pocket. He covered the twelve yards to the goal in four long strides. There he found his move covered by an alert defender, but that was expected. Tod half faked to his right, checked, and cut back to his left, aiming for the spot where he knew the pass was coming. Another Skeeter back was there with him, and both went up for the ball at the same instant. It was Tod's strong fingers that gripped it, holding on even when his opponent hacked his arm. And he hung on as they toppled across the white line of the goal.

The whole Cowboy crowd was up and yelling by the time he regained his feet.

"You all right, Tod?" Flick whispered in his ear. "This may be a close game, and I'd like to go for two."

"I'm OK. Sure—where do you want me?"

"Out toward the sideline. I'll throw hard and low."

Tod nodded, and the team lined up. The crowd saw that they weren't going to place-kick, and the yelling redoubled. Flick held up a hand for quiet. Finally he had to ask the referee's help, and the roar subsided. On the snap signal Tod swung to his right, running his hardest. He was one step ahead of the opposing end when the ball came at him like a bullet. He jumped, took the pass in his stomach, clutching it with both hands. The tackler was on him then, but he managed to fall sidewise, over the line. And the score was Prairie, eight—Skipton, seven.

The rest of that first quarter was a matter of fierce attack and hard-nosed defense. The Skeeters were full of surprises, but each time they pulled a new trick out of the hat, the home team managed to keep it in check. Reverses were nailed after short gains. Long passes were batted down by defending backs. And the line, charging like demons, stopped plunge after plunge.

Skipton ground out two first downs but was forced to punt from midfield. Flick took the kick on the three and reached the ten before they tackled him. Three cracks at the line by burly Aaron Weil picked up a first down, and Joe Luke made five more yards around end. There the attack stalled.

152

An incomplete forward pass was followed by a blitz that buried Flick on his own twenty. There the Cowboys, in turn, had to punt. The whistle ending the quarter found the Skeeters in possession of the ball on their own thirty-five.

The very first play looked like an end around, with the ballcarrier coming straight for Tod's position. But as he charged in to make the tackle, he saw the ball deftly handed off to a back, who scuttled wide around the opposite end. Rudy Ryker, like the rest of the defense, was fooled on the play, and before he could get untracked, the man with the ball was past him, streaking up the sideline. It was Flick, at safety, who finally stopped him. But by that time he was well past midfield.

The Skipton team had momentum now, and when their fullback crashed the line off tackle, he kept on going for another first down. Wisely Flick Davis asked the officials for a time-out.

"You guys are a little off balance," he told the team. "That trick play upset you. Now you've got two minutes to get organized again, and I hope the Skeeters'll cool off. Just remember you know how to play football as well as they do. Every man carry out his assignment an' we'll stop their drive."

The advice worked well on the first play and again on the second. Skipton had hit the line both times and gained only three yards in all. Now it was third down and seven to go— almost certainly a pass play, Tod thought.

Sure enough, when the ball was snapped, the quarterback pretended to hand it off to his fullback, then dodged behind him, looking for a downfield receiver. A second later he tucked the ball under his arm and sprinted toward the far sideline.

"Keeper!" yelled the Cowboys, and their linebackers shifted over in a hurry to nail the runner. But to Tod's chagrin, the quarterback stopped, turned, and threw a long pass diagonally over toward the opposite corner. The Skeeter left end had slipped past unobserved, and now he caught the ball on the five, diving over for a touchdown.

Tod was fiercely angry at himself. He joined the grim-faced team, and they lined up on the goal line to await the conversion.

"Hey—look!" said Joe Luke. "They're goin' for two!"

It appeared to be a pass, but the quarterback found his men covered and started to scramble. He was headed toward Tod's end. All Tod's pent-up frustration went into his tackle, and the ballcarrier was slammed down, a yard short of pay dirt. Now the score was Skipton, thirteen—Prairie, eight.

The Cowboys took the kickoff and proceeded to hammer out three first downs, getting as far as the Skipton forty. Flick had been jarred once or twice when the linebackers broke through to blitz him, and his passing wasn't as accurate as usual. With a third down and four to go, he tried a long one to Tod that was far off the mark. An alert Skeeter back intercepted it on his own five and ran it out ten yards before Tod could overtake him.

Bitterly disappointed, the Prairie players clenched their teeth and dug in to stop the visitors once more. Both teams were tired now, but Skipton had the advantage of having the ball and being in the lead. They hit hard, again and again, and made a few yards nearly every time. With two minutes left in the half, they were past the fifty. And there the quarterback took a daring third-down chance. He sent four receivers downfield and heaved a forty-yard bomb over the middle. It was a good pass, and it was aimed right between two of his men. Before a defender could get there, both Skeeters went up for the ball, each trying to catch it for himself. It bobbled from one to the other and finally fell to the turf as the whistle blew. The referee signaled "incomplete."

With fourth down now, the Skipton place-kicker was sent

in to try a long one. It was far too short, and Flick Davis sprinted back with it past the twenty. There he was content to run out the clock with safe line plunges, so Skipton retained its five-point lead as the weary elevens left the field.

None of the Cowboy players had a word to say. They slumped on the locker-room benches, their faces sullen with dejection. Dutch Kleinschmidt let them rest a few minutes, then started talking to them.

"The next time we're all together here," he said, "this game will be in the record books. Either Prairie or Skipton will be listed as the winner of the Tri-County championship. I know it means a lot to you, as it does to me. To look at some of you, a stranger would think you'd already lost. But you haven't! Five points isn't enough against a team like yours. Skipton knows it, even if you don't. They're worrying right now about how to stop the next touchdown you're going to make. Think that over while I have a talk with Flick."

He took the quarterback aside, and the rest of them sat up a little straighter, heartened by what he had said. Five minutes before time to go out, a familiar figure entered the locker room. It was Andy Willis, and he strutted down the aisle to his locker with his white teeth showing in a grin.

"Hi!" he greeted them. "Doc says I can get dressed this half. Even if I can't be in there with you, I want to sit on the bench an' watch you win!"

As he stripped, they saw the wide bandage of adhesive tape around his chest and middle.

"Does it hurt much?" Chris Olsen asked.

"Not much, any more. Only if I bend the wrong way. Mostly it just itches, an' boy—that drives me crazy!"

He put on his pads, got into his jersey and pants, and leaned over to tie his football shoes. "Ouch!" he said. "Somebody want to give me a hand?"

They all started to help, but Tod was nearest. Quickly he pulled the laces tight and tied the knots. "We sure miss you, Andy," he said. "With you in there, we'd really show 'em!"

An official came to the door and blew his whistle. In a moment they were filing out, their cleats clattering on the cement. It was time to start the second half.

17

Andy followed the squad out on the field. And last of all came the coach and Flick Davis, still talking strategy.

Tod felt rested now and calm. He knew he was ready to play as he had never played before, and he hoped all the others felt the same way. They were greeted by a long yell for the team. Then Mary Ann Foster must have caught sight of the little end, for she called for a cheer for Andy Willis. He waved in pleased embarrassment and went to sit on the bench.

The first eleven warmed up with some bodily contact exercises and ran out to receive the kickoff. A chilly Kansas wind had begun to blow, and little spirals of dust came whirling into their faces. The Skipton kicker teed up the ball, only to have it blown over. After another try one of the linemen moved up to hold it for him.

Tod saw the ball start its long ascent and knew it would be a deep kick. He hung back to block a tackler, but there was no runback. The wind took the ball and sailed it over Flick's head—over the goal line and clear out of the end zone.

It was brought out to the twenty, and there, after a huddle, the Cowboys lined up. The first play was a plunge by

Aaron Weil that covered seven yards. Then Joe Luke took it on a cross buck and battled his way for four more and a first down.

With a little more running room now, Flick faked another line play to the fullback and ran a keeper sweep around right end, with Tod blocking for him. Before he was tackled, he reached the forty-one, very close to another first down. The referee called for the sticks, and while the measurement was being taken, Flick pulled Tod aside.

"How about a lonesome end pass?" he asked. "After this play, stay out there and try to act invisible. Then go about thirty yards down, an' I'll get it to you."

A yell of joy from the Prairie rooting section told them the first down had been made. The team huddled in a hurry, and the quarterback called for another Weil plunge over guard. This time it only went for a couple of yards, but Tod wasn't watching. He had walked quietly out to the right and stood close to the sideline.

For a moment he thought he was unobserved, but just as Flick finished barking signals, two backfield men came drifting over in his direction. All he could do was run his pattern and hope for the best.

The two men were right on him when he saw the ball coming. Flick had realized he was in trouble, and the throw came high and fast. With all the spring in his legs, Tod jumped. His fingers were outstretched, but before the ball touched them, he was knocked down by a vicious tackle. He heard whistles blowing. By the time he caught his breath and stood up, he saw the officials placing the ball on the Skeeters' thirty-five-yard line. Pass interference had been called!

Flick was there at his elbow. "Sorry!" he said. "Are you hurt? I had to get rid of it, an' I figured the best way was to throw over you."

"Heck—I'm OK!" Tod told him. "If they hadn't downed me, I might have caught it at that. But the play didn't fool

158

'em. I'm pretty sure they must have scouted some of our games."

In the huddle Flick called for an end sweep, with two other backs blocking ahead of Joe Luke. Unfortunately the play went around left end, and Rudy Ryker stumbled right in front of the blockers. They all went down in a heap, and only Joe's quickness in cutting inside prevented a big loss.

With a second down and nine to go, the coach sent in a substitute guard with instructions for a pass. "OK," Flick told them. "Tod—straight ahead ten yards, then cut to your left."

This time the play went as planned. Tod ran forward across two five-yard stripes, dodged a corner-back, and spun to his left. The pass came to him straight as an arrow, and he had time for a stride toward the goal line before he was tackled. It was first down now, on the enemy's twenty-two.

Flick looked over the defense coolly. The suceesss of that pass had made the Skeeters angry, and he was sure they would try to blitz him on the next play. Faking beautifully, he took the ball from center, tucked it quickly into Weil's midriff, and ran back, hiding his right arm as if he had the ball and was looking for a receiver.

The big fullback crouched over and waited till the Skeeter guards and linebackers had time to charge past him, then went plowing through the hole they had left. While Flick was being snowed under, Weil reached the ten before the safety man downed him. Then Skipton called for a time-out to try to reorganize their defense.

"All right, guys," Flick panted to his teammates. "We've got four downs to cross that last stripe. They'll be lined up, seven men abreast on the line. So how do we fool 'em? A pass? No, they may be lookin' for that, too. Tod, you cross the goal line, an' if you're open, I'll throw to you. If you're covered, I'll scramble for it. OK, everybody?"

All of them agreed. With the end of the time-out, they lined up strong to the left, and the Skeeters shifted nervously in the same direction. At the snap Tod took off for the goal. Out of the corner of his eye, he could see the Skipton line charging hard in an effort to trap the passer. He turned and waved his arms, drawing the defensive backs to cover him. Then he saw Flick dart out to the right, swivel away from the clutch of the end, and turn on speed as he made for the corner. The next instant he was over for the touchdown!

The team huddled, waiting for the wild yelling of the crowd to quiet a little. There was no reason, Flick told them, to go for a two-pointer, for they now led, fourteen to thirteen. A place-kick would give them a two-point edge. The line held firm, and Aaron Weil's well-trained toe put the ball squarely between the uprights.

Fifteen to thirteen wasn't really much of a lead, as the Cowboys knew. Most of the second half still had to be played, and Skipton wasn't a team to give up easily. Furthermore, the strain of playing both offense and defense had begun to tell on the Prairie eleven. They kicked off to a well-rested offensive team, then dug in doggedly to hold the attackers.

The strong contingent of Skipton fans roared encouragement from their side of the field, and the Skeeters responded by making a first down in three line plays. Once they were out to the thirty-five, their quarterback unlimbered his passing arm. Two short tosses in succession took them to the midfield stripe, and the Prairie rooters began to yell, "Get that ball!"

Varying the attack, the Skipton signal-caller sent his fullback over tackle, but Mike Hoban stopped him cold. Then they tried the other side, and Chris Olsen was equally effective in dumping the ballcarrier. With a third down and nine to go, the Skeeters called for a time-out. It gave them a chance to plan new strategy, but it also brought the Cowboys a welcome breather.

160

"They've just about got to pass," Flick told his men. "You backs better be ready to cover any receiver. And you guys in the line—pile through to blitz him if you can."

The play certainly started like a forward pass, but just as the wave of linemen roared through to swamp the passer, the ball was lateraled out to a hard-running halfback. He flashed past the slower-footed Ryker and dodged Tony Fortunato's tackle. Before Flick could bring him down, he had reached the Prairie twenty-yard line.

The Cowboys huddled again, weary but determined to stop the drive. They held a line-plunge for no gain, then knocked down an attempted pass. The third-down play was another lateral that almost succeeded. But this time it came around Tod's end, and he made a desperate dive that caught the ballcarrier on the fifteen.

Now, with fourth down and five to go, the Skeeters lined up in field-goal formation. The angle was from one side, but they had the wind with them. And Tod remembered with a sinking heart that they had one of the best place-kickers in the state. The man measured the distance with care and stood ready while the quarterback knelt to hold the ball.

The Cowboy line charged furiously, trying to block the kick, but the ball soared past their reaching hands. It went up in a clean arc, barely missed the left upright, and went through for a three-point score.

Naturally the yelling from the Skipton rooters was deafening. Their team was ahead once more—sixteen to fifteen!

Perhaps, Tod thought, the Prairie eleven should have gone for a two-point conversion. But who wanted a tie! No, they just had to fight for another touchdown. That was in all their minds as they got into position to take the kickoff. It came down, borne on the wind, and carried over the goal line as before.

Flick had time to call only one play before the period

ended. It was a line buck over tackle, good for five yards. They started the final quarter with a second down on their own twenty-five.

*   *   *

The wind came stronger now, and clouds darkened the sky. The Prairie boys shivered and thrashed their arms as they huddled before play was resumed. Flick had run over to the sideline to talk to the coach.

"Not much we can do," he told the team when he returned, "except keep possession of that ball. We've got to hammer out first downs till we're in striking distance. It's second and five. Aaron, you'll hit over guard on the first play. All right—there's the whistle. Let's go!"

The Cowboys' fans, undaunted, gave a long yell for the team as they lined up. Then the battle was on again. Aaron Weil carried for four, hitting the same spot a moment later and making the first down.

An end sweep by Joe Luke gained only a couple of yards. Flick tried a short pass to Todd, but a gust of wind twisted it out of his reach. On third down the speedy quarterback faked another pass, and once the defenders were committed, he scrambled, taking the ball all the way to the forty-five. There two linebackers hit him from opposite sides, and a third man piled on after he was down. The referee flung down his flag and called a personal foul, which delighted the hometown fans.

A moment later their joy turned to consternation, for Flick didn't get up. Tod ran to his side and was quickly joined by Mike Hoban and Dutch Kleinschmidt. Flick's eyes were open, but his face was twisted in pain.

"It—it's my knee!" he panted. "Hurts like crazy when I try to bend it."

A doctor hurried from the stands. He felt the injured leg and shook his head gravely. "Get a stretcher," he said. "This

162

boy's through playing for today. That piling on must have wrenched some ligaments."

There was heavy silence on both sides of the field as the Cowboys' quarterback was carried to the gym. From the bench the coach brought his scrub signal-caller, a youngster named Willie Fretz, who had never played a varsity game in his life. He was nervous and scared, but the rest of the team talked to him, trying to build his confidence.

The ball, after the stiff penalty, was now in Skipton territory, on the forty-yard line. In the huddle Mike Hoban, the co-captain, told Fretz what play to call.

"All you've got to do, Willie, is hand off to Aaron. Pancho an' I'll give him a hole to go through. I know you're jumpy now, but after the first play you'll settle down. OK?"

In a quavering voice the boy called a string of signals, then clutched the ball Link Carey thrust at him and promptly dropped it. The fullback fell on it before enemy hands could reach it, and the loss on the play was only a yard.

"Come on, kid," Tod told the young substitute. "Just forget it's a game. You handle plenty o' balls in practice. Now try it again."

This time the hand-off went more smoothly, but Aaron made only three yards, and it was third down, with eight to go. At a signal from the bench, Mike asked for a time-out and hurried over to talk to the coach. When he returned, he brought the scrub right end with him. Finley Baker was a tall, lanky farm boy, slow of speech but quick enough on the field.

"Tod," said the big tackle, "Dutch wants you to take over at quarter. Baker'll play in your place. Fretz, you go back to the bench till you're needed again. We've got to pass on this down."

It was a patchy lineup, as Tod well knew. But somehow they had to make it work.

"All right," he told them in the huddle, "I'm going to pass to Joe Luke, over the middle. Finley, you head downfield an' try to draw off the defense. Now let's get us a first down!"

Crouching over center, he breathed a small prayer that he might steady the team. Then he had the ball and was back-pedaling while Joe Luke plunged through the line. An avalanche of orange shirts roared toward him, but his eyes were on Luke. At the last possible instant, he let fly with his pass, then ducked to meet the rush of blitzing Skeeters.

It wasn't until he picked himself off the turf that he knew what had happened. The ball was being placed somewhere around the thirty, and the pass had been good.

"Where's the ball?" he gasped to Mike Hoban.

"First an' ten on the twenty-nine!" Mike told him happily. "That was a dandy pass! You all right?"

"Sure—but I've found out what a beating poor Flick has to take. What'll we do now—hit the line again?"

The rest of them agreed, and on the hand-off Aaron plowed ahead for a gain to the twenty-five. Another try was held for only two yards, and they faced a third down with a tough four yards to go. Tod was worried as he went toward the huddle. He wondered if he could pass successfully again, with the Skeeters laying for him.

Then, suddenly, he was aware of a new figure running onto the field. There was a hush, then a wild howl of joy from the Prairie rooters. The newcomer was little Andy Willis, his grin as bright as his clean uniform.

18

"The coach figures I'm good for one play," the fleetfooted end told them. "Sorry, Rudy, but I'm s'posed to take your place at left end. Where you want me to run to, Tod?"

"I reckon you'd better go straight ahead, then cut to your right," said Tod. "They'll be in on me, but I'll dodge loose if I can. Good luck, Andy—an' try not to get hurt!"

As they lined up, it was obvious that the Skipton defense knew what was coming. Tod saw the corner-backs shifting to cover Andy, and he changed his signals to call for a pass to the right end. Young Finley Baker looked up, startled, but Tod went right on barking numbers.

At his final "Hup!" he took the ball from Carey and darted back, slipping away from the charging linemen. Over their heads he could see three defenders clustered around Andy. But Baker was in the clear. Tod threw a perfect pitch—a soft, arching spiral that would be easy to catch. And the young end lived up to his hopes. He took the ball on the ten-yard line and clung to it tightly when he was tackled on the five.

In the huddle Andy Willis was chuckling. "You crossed me up, boy!" he said. "But it was a good thing you did.

Too many o' those pesky Skeeters on me. Last thing we want is an interception!"

"Sorry, Andy," Tod told him. "I wanted you to be the hero. Now we've got a real chance to put it over. What do you say, gang?"

"Let me carry," said Weil. "I can come close, and we've got four downs to do it."

"Hold on," Tod answered. "They'll expect just that, Aaron, and they'll line up solid to stop you. I doubt if they'll be looking for another pass. Andy, maybe you won't be covered this time. How about edging over to the goal line for a quick one?"

"Yes, *sir!*" said the little speedster. "Throw it quick as you get it. I'll be there!"

The Cowboys could smell victory now, and they had a new eagerness. It cost them a five-yard penalty when Pancho Villa charged off side. But when they huddled again, they all agreed to let the play go as planned.

The stands were silent as Tod called his signals. He took the pigskin and pretended to slap it into Weil's midriff, and the fullback plunged hard, with his arms folded as if he had the ball. Tod could see Andy sprinting goalward, and he jumped high, rifling the ball toward a spot just beyond the flying end.

Before it reached its mark, Tod was knocked down, but the frenzied cheers from the Prairie side of the field told him Andy must have made the catch. Mike Hoban pulled Tod to his feet and hugged him. "We got us a touchdown, boy!" he was babbling ecstatically.

They huddled, facing the sullen Skeeter line. "How do the ribs feel, Andy?" asked Tod.

"Mighty sore. They kind o' put the squeeze on me," he panted, and Tod could see him wince as he felt his chest.

"OK, we'll play it safe," said the makeshift quarterback.

166

"Hold the line, everybody, an' give Aaron a chance to kick the point."

He knelt, waiting for the pass from center. When it came, he juggled it for a split second but got it down in time. And Weil, steady as ever, kicked it high over the crossbar.

Tired as he was, Tod's heart lifted to the roar from his hometown folks. The score was Prairie, twenty-two; Skipton, sixteen.

As the Cowboys trudged back to kick off, Tod ran to the sideline where the official timekeeper stood.

"How many minutes to go?" he asked.

"Four minutes, twenty-five seconds," was the curt reply. But the man gave him a friendly grin as he spoke.

The team huddled briefly. "Well, gang," Tod told them. "All we've got to do now is keep 'em from scoring in the next four minutes and a half. How about it?"

Most of them were too weary to waste breath and simply nodded. But Rudy Ryker, now back in on defense, grunted a "You bet!"

With the freshening wind at his back, Aaron Weil didn't kick it high, for he knew it would carry too far. Instead, he kept the ball low and put a lot of power behind it. It went whirling just over the linemen's heads, bounced once, and spun on—an almost impossible ball to catch.

Tod, hanging back in safety position, saw an orange-shirted player make a grab for it, knock it sidewise, and make an ineffectual dive to recover it. And Rudy Ryker, who had gone galloping down under the kick, pounced on the loose ball.

The Prairie crowd went crazy. Some had been worrying about holding the Skeeter attack—wondering if the six-point lead would stand up. Now they saw a chance to stretch that lead, and they yelled themselves hoarse. When Tod reached the huddle, all the other players were hugging the big end and pounding him on the back. "Attaboy, Rudy! Great play, kid!" they panted.

Now the sticks were being moved, and Tod saw that they would be starting from the Skipton nineteen-yard line. Before he could outline the play, there was a fresh roar from the crowd, and Andy Willis trotted out on the field, replacing the defensive hero at left end.

"Coach says pass quick," he told Tod, "while they're still discombobulated!"

Tod nodded. He had had the same idea, and now that Andy was back, he had a first-class receiver.

"Finley," he asked the young right end, "do you reckon you can fool 'em—make 'em think I'm passing to you?"

"I'll try," said the boy.

"OK, then—here goes."

He began calling signals, his steady voice calming the tension they all felt. Baker, the gangling youngster, started at the snap and ran hard toward the goal line, looking back and gesturing with his arms. Tod sidestepped the blitzing linemen and pretended to scramble to the right. Then, as he was about to be tackled, he let fly with a cross-field pass that found Andy in the clear on the five-yard line. The little end made the catch, darted over, and was brought down hard, after crossing the last stripe.

Every man on the Prairie team gathered around him where he lay, his face contorted with pain. They would have carried him to the bench, but Tod insisted they should wait for the doctor. It was well they did, for Andy was suffering badly.

"Got those ribs again," he gasped through set teeth. "But we scored! Now I've got all winter to heal up!"

There was a time-out while the doctor examined him. Then he was placed on a stretcher and carried to the gym. And as soon as he reached the sideline, the whistle blew to resume play. Rudy Ryker had come back, his sturdy bulk

168

buttressing the left side of the line. And Tod called for a placement to make the extra point. Aaron Weil grinned and stepped back into position for the kick. A moment later he had put the ball over.

Somebody had rigged up a scoreboard at one end of the field, and now the figures on it read: Cowboys, 29—Visitors, 16. They had, as Mike Hoban said, "put the icing on the cake."

The heart seemed to have gone out of the Skeeters. They took the kickoff only as far as the eighteen-yard line, and there their attack bogged down. After three tries they failed to make a first down and had to punt against the wind. Joe Luke caught it near midfield and ran it back to the Visitors' forty. But before the Prairie eleven could call a play, the gun sounded, ending the game.

*   *   *

Tod thought he had never been so tired in his life. Yet the thrill of victory put spring in his step as he pushed through the mob of admirers, trying to make his way to the locker room.

His father and Mrs. McDonald caught up with him just as he reached the gym door.

"Pretty good game," Jim Ross growled. But his delighted grin betrayed his real emotions. The housekeeper flung her arms around Tod in a powerful hug. She was dressed in her Sunday best, but her flowered hat hung rakishly over one eye.

"No such thing!" she exclaimed with vehemence. "It was a *great* game! Now I gotta go find that Mary Dennis 'fore she sneaks off. But don't you folks worry—I'll have supper ready for you!"

Coach Kleinschmidt was waiting just inside, greeting the players as they entered. His big hand seized Tod's arm in a crushing grip. "Boy," he said, "you sure came through when we needed you!" And his choking voice told Tod how deeply he meant it.

"How's Flick?" Tod asked. "And how's Andy?"

"The doc says Flick'll be fine in a couple of weeks if he keeps off that foot. Andy's ribs may take a bit longer to heal. But they're both too happy to care!"

There was some raucous singing as the boys showered. And tired as they were, they couldn't get dressed without a bit of horseplay. Mike Hoban was one of the most boisterous, but when they were ready to leave, he sobered up enough to tell Tod some news.

"Did you hear about those two cattle rustlers?" he asked. "Both of 'em pleaded guilty at the hearing. They come up for sentencing next week, so there'll be no trial, an' I reckon we won't have to testify. We ought to be gettin' the reward pretty quick. What'll you do with the money?"

"I haven't had much chance to think about it. Put it in the bank an' save it for college, maybe. How about you?"

Mike squirmed a little. "Well," he admitted, "I thought I might buy me a little sports car. Maybe your idea makes more sense, but I'm hopin' to get an athletic scholarship next fall."

"Gee!" said Tod. "I never thought o' that. I bet they'll be trying to get you all right."

They drove home together in the pickup truck. The reaction from the game had set in, and they were both too tired to talk any more. Tod stumbled into the house, pulled off his boots, and flung himself down on the bed. That was the last he knew until his father woke him at seven o'clock.

"Supper's on the table," he said, "an' I reckon you can eat, after the way you worked to win that game."

As soon as Tod was fully awake, he found his father was right. He was ravenously hungry, and Mrs. McDonald had prepared plenty of good food.

At eight, Jim Ross turned on the television set to a local channel that carried the sports roundup.

"Well, folks," the commentator said, "they finally settled that Tri-County football championship this afternoon. If you weren't there, you missed a good one. The Prairie Cowboys not only had to come from behind to beat Skipton, but they did it by two touchdowns—twenty-nine to sixteen. What made their victory more surprising was that they lost their star quarterback, Flick Davis, in the second half and had to use an end to do the passing and signal calling. He's a lanky kid named Tod Ross, who—believe it or not—is playing his first year of football! In the off season he puts in his time roping calves and rounding up cattle rustlers. More power to Coach Dutch Kleinschmidt and his new champs!"

Mrs. Mack had come to the door to listen, and she stood there beaming. "How do you like that!" she remarked loudly. "Guess that makes us famous 'round here, Tod!"

Embarrassed, he tried to belittle the telecast, but his father made no effort to conceal his pride.

"Don't know what ailed me," he chuckled, "when I undertook to keep you from playin' football! Musta been touched in the head!"

At that moment the telephone rang, and Jim Ross went to answer it.

"Who?" Tod heard him say. "Oh—you want to talk to the hero? Hang on a minute."

Tod took the receiver, frowning at his father, but the happy voice that came over the wire brought a grin to his face.

"Hi!" said Mary Ann. "I tried to catch you when you went off the field, but your father was there first, along with that big woman in the funny hat."

Tod laughed. "Don't be scared o' her," he said. "That's our housekeeper, Mrs. McDonald."

"Well," the girl replied, "she did look sort of forbidding. Tod, did you listen to the sports news on TV?"

"Yeah. He laid it on pretty thick. I'll be ashamed to go to school Monday!"

"Why, Tod! Every word was true, and you know it. But that isn't the only reason I wanted to call you. They're getting the fairgrounds pavilion fixed up, and the 4-H judging is going to be the Friday after Thanksgiving. So can you come and help me with Buttercup that day? It'll be in the afternoon this time, but maybe you can stay for dinner afterward."

"Thanks," Tod told her. "I'd like to come. How's your calf doing these days, Mary Ann?"

"I may be prejudiced, but I think she's prettier than ever, and I work on her every day so her coat looks gorgeous. I'm glad you can come, Tod, and I'll be seeing you in school. 'By, now."

Tod looked at the calendar on the wall. It was nearly two weeks to Thanksgiving. He'd have plenty of time to get a haircut and maybe buy a new jacket before going to dinner at the Fosters'.

On Monday morning when Mike picked him up in the little truck, Tod had to take some more ribbing about the broadcast.

"Sure—you deserved it," the big tackle told him. "But there were ten or eleven other guys playin', too. The dope never mentioned that most of us played every minute of the game—offense an' defense both."

"Right," said Tod. "I thought that was the real story. An' why didn't he give Andy some credit—catching that pass with most of his ribs busted? Oh, well—at least the sports writers know Prairie's on the map, now."

172

19

Tod tried to make himself small and inconspicuous when he took his seat in the classroom. But he could hear a buzz of whispers among the girls. Then Tony Fortunato spotted him and gave him a wink and an elaborate bow.

Dutch Kleinschmidt rapped for order, but his stern face broke into a little smile when he caught sight of Tod. He, too, must have heard the sportscast. At the end of the period, he made an announcement.

"There's going to be a dinner for the football team a week from tonight," he said. "The Chamber of Commerce is giving it, in the main dining room at the Prairie House. I want the whole squad to be there."

"Hey!" Tony called to Tod as they went out into the corridor. "You think that means they'll be giving us the new equipment they said they would?"

"Not right off. You know they've got to raise the money first."

"Why? How much do new uniforms cost?"

"I don't know," Tod told him, "but I'd say at least a hundred bucks for each player, if you count shoes an' helmet. That might run to around three thousand dollars!"

Not much else was talked about in school that day. Everyone was proud of the Cowboys, and the coming dinner would be discussed in homes all through the area. Tickets would surely go like hot cakes.

Flick Davis and Andy Willis were both back in school in spite of their injuries. Flick's knee had been tightly bandaged, and he was on crutches, but he claimed it didn't hurt much. Andy was in more pain, though nobody would have known it. All he had to do, he said, was stay away from people who made funny remarks. Laughing nearly killed him.

It seemed strange not to go to the gym when classes ended for the day. But for this week, at least, the athletes would have a rest. Basketball practice didn't start in earnest till after the Thanksgiving holiday.

"How about it?" said Mike as Tod got into the truck. "Your folks goin' to the dinner?"

"I'd like to see anybody try to keep my dad away. I bet your father an' mother'll want to be there, too—to see you get honored."

Mike grinned sheepishly. "Yeah," he said. "Just so I don't have to make a speech! You think we'll get anything besides a free feed?"

"If they give us those uniforms, that's all I want."

When he got home, Tod found his father out in the feed lot. "Did you hear about the football banquet, Pa?" he asked.

Jim Ross nodded. "I was there when the Chamber o' Commerce voted on it," he replied.

"We all think it's a swell idea," Tod told him. "Just one thing, though—how many can they get in the dining room at the hotel?"

"About a hundred, I reckon. Why?"

"I'll bet there'll be five hundred that would like to go. The whole territory around Prairie seems to be mighty proud about our being champs."

174

"So what? The Prairie House is the biggest place we can find."

"But, Pa—does it have to be so quick? The pavilion at the fairgrounds'll be all fixed up by Thanksgiving, an' that would hold a lot more folks."

"Hm," his father mused. "Maybe you're right. Nobody'd lose interest if we put it off a week. I hear the 4-H kids'll be there the day after Thanksgiving. But the place could be cleaned up an' tables put in by Monday night. I guess I'll call the committee right now."

Before that evening was over, Tod's idea had been adopted enthusiastically by the Chamber of Commerce. The only dissenting vote, naturally, was that of the Prairie House proprietor.

"Hey, man!" said Mike when he took Tod aboard the next morning. "I hear you got 'em to move that football banquet back a week."

"All I did was make a remark to my father, an' he carried on from there. But don't you agree it's better to have more people interested?"

"Sure! I guess I can wait a bit longer. It'll take some hard work to get the pavilion ready, though."

At noon there was a student meeting. Motions were made, a vote was taken, and before he knew what was happening, Tod was elected chairman of a high-school committee to work with the Chamber of Commerce. They all yelled for him to make a speech.

When he got up, red-faced, he waited for the hubbub to quiet down. "OK," he said, "I'll take the job if you're all willing to pitch in an' help. Let's see, now. Somebody's got to organize teams to sell tickets. I'll appoint Aaron Weil to do that. Then we've got to have forty or fifty boys ready to work in the pavilion after the 4-H animals are out. You'll take care o' that, Mike. An' we'll need lots o' good food cooked an' served. I nominate Mary Ann Foster an' her home economics girls to see we get fed."

There had been no time to plan any of this, but as one idea after another popped into his head, he delegated the authority to people he knew he could trust. Posters and banners, for example, were turned over to students in the art class. And the best part of it was that the various chairmen were all eager to get to work.

Half an hour later, as he sat in English class, a feeling of amazement came over Tod. All his life he had thought of himself as independent of others, completely self-sufficient. And here, all of a sudden, he was running a big school function. It made him humble. Maybe, he thought, it was playing on the football team that had made him see the value of working with other people.

He was busier, the rest of that week, than he had ever been before. After school each day, he got his chairmen together and checked up on their efforts. Then in the evenings, he had to attend committee meetings of the town's businessmen in company with his father. Jim Ross supported everything he did and helped him keep the fires of enthusiasm burning. On Friday night, as they drove home after a long session, the rancher said a surprising thing.

"You know, son," he remarked, "I've always been stand-offish. Figured I'd rather paddle my own canoe. But this is sort of fun. By thunder, I believe you'd make a good politician—the way you can kid folks along an' get 'em to do what you want!"

Tod shook his head. "No politics for me!" he answered. "I'd rather raise cattle."

Saturday was no holiday for him. There had been some questions about the pavilion as a place to hold the banquet, and he felt he had to see for himself. As he rode his pony toward the fairgrounds, he heard hoofs pounding behind

176

him and looked back. Mary Ann Foster was galloping after him, her yellow hair flying.

"Hi!" she called. "I was getting ready to go to the fairgrounds when I saw you go by. You going to look over the pavilion?"

"That's right. I want to see how much space we'll have."

She told him her girls were all organized to do the cooking and wait on the tables. "I thought I might have trouble getting them to work," she said. "But every one of them wants to be on the team!"

"I know," Tod answered with a grin. "Aaron's found the same thing. The kids can't wait for the tickets to come from the printers. An' there isn't a store in town that won't be proud to have a poster in the window!"

The new metal roof of the pavilion at the fairgrounds gleamed in the sun as they rode up. They tied their horses to the fence and found a small door that was unlocked. Inside, the huge circular room was cold and echoing with emptiness.

"That's the first thing I want to make sure of—heat," said Tod. "It's liable to be freezing weather. Let's take a look."

They found a little heater room off at one side and traced the hot-water pipes that ran all the way around the building just above the floor. A boiler, heated by natural gas, was evidently the source of warmth for the whole pavilion. To Mary Ann's delight there was also a completely equipped kitchen. It had been put in, she explained, to accommodate the cooking contests for the 4-H girls.

"Look at those ovens!" she said proudly. "We could cook twenty turkeys at a time, or twenty big roasts of beef!"

"Which do you plan to have?" Tod asked.

"Well, we thought it was too soon after Thanksgiving for turkey," she told him. "But everybody likes roast beef."

He nodded. "All right," he said. "You go on and check your kitchen equipment. "I've got to measure the amount o' room we'll have."

He paced carefully from one side of the room to the other. It came out about thirty-five yards—roughly a hundred feet. Then, with a pencil and paper he started laying out table arrangements. The head table, seating about twelve important people, would be close to one wall. In front of it, as close together as they could be placed while still allowing space for the waitresses to move, twenty-five more tables would fit, he figured, seating ten each. That meant they could handle over two hundred and fifty guests, which was actually more than he had hoped.

Stored in a sort of shed, off the pavilion, he found enough trestle tables to seat that many. They were ordinarily used for displaying jams, jellies, cakes, and other baked goods entered by the 4-H contestants. But only about a hundred folding chairs could be located. More would have to be borrowed from the town's two funeral parlors.

"Hey, Mary Ann," he called. "Come take a look at this."

He showed her the sketch he had drawn. "Twenty-five tables with ten at each table. You girls are going to be plenty busy!"

"Wow!" she exclaimed. "Can you really get that many in?"

"I'm pretty sure we can, but it'll take a lot o' getting ready. Saturday an' Sunday we'll have to get half the school out here. I'll give Mike a call. He's in charge o' that job."

When he got home, he was on the telephone most of the evening. Aaron Weil was told how many diners could be accommodated, and he promised to have his ticket sellers at work by Monday. Mike agreed that they would need at least thirty boys on hand the next weekend, to clean up the 4-H judging area and set up the tables. He also offered to

178

see the funeral directors and talk them into furnishing the chairs free.

One more call, to the art teacher, brought him the news that twenty posters were already made and as many more would be forthcoming. And last but not least, Tod's father told him he had arranged to have a long banner lettered and stretched across Main Street, where nobody could miss it.

*　　*　　*

The first three days of Thanksgiving week were still busy ones for Tod. He was called on to straighten out a few difficulties and keep a constant check on the progress made by his various committee leaders. He even had to miss a meeting of the football squad, called for Tuesday afternoon. But by Wednesday he felt everything was running smoothly. He put it all out of his mind, slept soundly, and rose late, ready to enjoy the holiday.

It was a dark, overcast morning. The north wind had a bite to it, and he found a thin skim of ice on the water in the cattle troughs. By ten o'clock it had started to snow.

"Good thing your football season ended when it did," his father remarked. "I wouldn't be surprised if we got half a foot 'fore we're done."

They spent a lazy day indoors and enjoyed the plump little turkey Mrs. McDonald had roasted. By nightfall the storm was abating, but four or five inches of snow had fallen. Tod had to put on galoshes when he went out to do the chores. The stars were shining overhead, and he could hear the drip of water from the eaves. Tomorrow, he thought, would see the snow melt fast.

Later in the evening he got a phone call from Mary Ann. "Tod," she said, "isn't this weather awful? I'm hoping for a clear day tomorrow because I have to be at the fairgrounds from ten o'clock on. They start judging the food early, and I've got a cake and some jelly entered. The calves won't be shown till two o'clock. You're still coming to see Buttercup, aren't you?"

"Sure—maybe I'll come earlier. Anything you want me to bring?"

"Just keep the calf and me company till the big moment. Thanks, Tod!"

He went to bed early and was up before dawn, as usual. With the chores done and breakfast eaten, he slicked up a little and put on his good clothes.

"Pa," he asked, "you need me this morning? I'd kind o' like to go over to the 4-H Fair."

Jim Ross looked at him sternly from under his craggy brows. "Hm!" he grunted. "Sort o' dressed up, aren't you? Wouldn't be a girl in it somewhere, would there?"

"Well, yeah. Mary Ann Foster's entered that calf o' hers."

"I don't reckon you'd be much use around here. Go ahead."

Tod saddled the buckskin, whistling while he worked. Most of the snow was already gone, the sun was bright, and the temperature had climbed to the middle forties. A number of cars passed him, headed toward town, and he had to stay well off the road to avoid being splashed. It was about ten-thirty when he hitched the pony outside and made his way into the pavilion.

At first he couldn't see Mary Ann in the crowd that filled the place. Then he caught a glimpse of her yellow hair, over by the baked goods table. As he drew closer, he saw a judge pinning a gold-lettered red ribbon on her sweater.

"Hi, Tod!" she hailed. "My coconut cake took a second!"

"Great!" he told her. "When do I get a piece?"

"Right now, if you'd like. The judges had to cut it, of course. Here, hold out your hand!"

"Yum!" he murmured around a luscious mouthful. "Don't see how you missed taking first!"

He followed her toward another long table, loaded with

180

sparkling jars of preserves. And after half an hour of suspense, while the three housewives acting as judges tasted and compared and smacked their lips, he saw the ribbons awarded. It pleased him that Mary Ann won first prize for her grape jelly, and a blue ribbon joined the red one on her sweater.

"There," she said happily, "now I feel better. You don't suppose my luck is all used up, do you? I do so want the calf to win something!"

A little before noon, the 4-H boys began clearing the tables out of the pavilion to make room for the livestock judging ring. The dairy calf class wouldn't be called for two hours, and Many Ann invited Tod to share her picnic lunch.

"I sort of hoped you'd be here, so I made a lot of extra sandwiches," she told him.

They had finished and were putting the paper cups and wrappings back in the hamper when Wade Foster arrived. He had brought Buttercup over in the truck, and for the next hour Tod helped Mary Ann brush down her sleek golden coat. In the brief time since he had seen her, the little heifer had grown and filled out, he thought. There was no question about it—she was beautiful.

By two o'clock the livestock ring had been set up, and the farmer-judges were ready. Calves of the beef breeds came first. They were led in by the boys who had raised them and lined up for inspection. Tod admired all seven of them, but his interest was naturally greatest in the white-faced Herefords—the same breed his father raised. The others were sleek black Angus and stocky Shorthorns. After half an hour of close examination, the judges picked two calves as outstanding, and finally gave the win to a solid, straight-backed Hereford.

"Now," Mary Ann breathed in Tod's ear, "it'll be our turn!"

There were only four dairy calves to be shown. They in-

181

cluded Buttercup and another Guernsey, a big black-and-white Holstein, and a spotted dark brown Ayrshire. All the owners stood by their calves, patting and encouraging them. Mary Ann was the only girl.

Tod stood back with the crowd and watched the judges as they sized up each entry in turn. To his own eyes Buttercup was a much prettier heifer than the other Guernsey, and apparently the judges thought so, too. After a few minutes they brought the two best ones forward—Buttercup and the tall Holstein. Then came the agonizing moment when they reached a decision. One man nodded to the other and went to the table where the ribbons lay. He brought back the red one first, and while Tod held his breath, it was pinned to the halter of the Holstein. The crowd cheered, and Mary Ann jumped up and down. The blue first-prize ribbon went to her little Guernsey.

Tod sprang forward to congratulate the girl and was suddenly caught in a warm embrace. There were tears in Mary Ann's eyes. "I guess," she said, "I must be the happiest girl in Kansas!"

20

Through the rest of that weekend, Tod worked like a galley slave. Just calling people on the phone didn't get things done. He had to be right on the scene.

By Sunday afternoon the floor of the pavilion had been scrubbed down, and the trestle tables were being set up. Tod found that the rough plan he had drawn was surprisingly accurate. Seating four on each side and one at each end would allow ten diners to a table. He even made extra room for the football squad right in front of the long speakers' table, then fanned out the others around the room.

The available chairs were put in place, but at the last minute he had to commandeer two trucks to go into town for the funeral parlor chairs. Meanwhile, the girls had been busy on their part of the job. They set the tables with bright paper place mats and little bouquets of chrysanthemums to give a festive look. Tod wanted to ask about the food they planned to serve, but he was promptly chased out of the kitchen.

"Don't you worry," Mary Ann told him. "There'll be enough to eat, and it'll be good, too."

Tod looked around to make sure he had done everything he could. As he started to leave, Aaron Weil came in.

"Boy, oh, boy!" cried the fullback. "This place looks good. But are you sure you've got enough seats? We sold out two hundred an' fifty tickets—not a one left."

Tod grinned. "Two hundred an' fifty—count 'em," he said. "We couldn't put in another table if we tried. I suppose you'll have to turn down a few latecomers tomorrow, but they had their chance."

At last he went home, satisfied there was no more to be done.

"You got your ticket, didn't you?" he asked his father.

Big Jim Ross nodded solemnly. "I got number four," he replied. "Happened to be there when the first batch came from the printers. You figure to have a full house?"

"Yep," Tod told him. "All sold out. Good night, Pa."

Monday was frosty, but clear. Mike picked him up as usual, and all they talked about was the big event that night.

"I hear they expect to clear 'round five hundred dollars," said Mike. "That'll help buy the new football equipment, won't it?"

"Yep, it'll help. But they need a lot more'n that. They'll have to raise the rest from the businessmen."

In school, Tod found it hard to concentrate on his lessons, and he wasn't the only one. The teachers found the lack of attention frustrating. More than once they had to reprimand a whole class for what appeared to be daydreaming. Only Dutch Kleinschmidt understood the restlessness of his charges. He called some of the football players together at noon and reminded them that they would be guests of honor at the dinner.

"Better get there early," he said. "There'll be a few speeches, but you won't have to talk. Just be ready to stand up and take a bow when your names are called."

The afternoon session ended at last, and the boys hurried home. No sooner was Tod in the house than his father handed him a letter.

"Came in today's mail," he said with a twinkle. "From the postmark, I reckon I know what's in it."

Tod tore open the envelope and found a check for twenty-five hundred dollars, made out in his name. It was signed by the treasurer of the Cattlemen's Association. He stared at it, and all he could whisper was, "Gosh!"

"It's a lot o' money," said his father. "But you earned it, so I won't tell you what to do with it. Better get dressed up, hadn't you? I'll let you drive me in the car."

The dinner was scheduled for six, like most such occasions in that part of the country, and the Rosses were there ten minutes early. Already the pavilion was beginning to fill with people. The girls, looking pretty in their waitress costumes, were doing last-minute things to the tables, and fresh-scrubbed boys were ushering the guests to their places.

As a member of the Chamber of Commerce, Jim Ross went to a seat at the long head table. And Tod found his own place card at one of the three tables reserved for the football squad.

Finally everyone was seated. Immediately they rose again while the Methodist minister asked the blessing. Then they fell to with a will. There were huge platters of roast beef, mountains of fluffy mashed potatoes, and plenty of brown gravy. There were green beans and corn, pickles and relishes, and plates of hot, fresh-baked biscuts, with butter and jam. The young people had milk and the grownups coffee. And last of all, the girls proudly brought in home-made ice cream and cakes they had baked themselves.

When everyone was filled almost to bursting, the president of the Chamber of Commerce rang with a spoon on a glass and stood up.

"Guess you all know why we're here," he began. "Prairie wants to do honor to a great football team—a team that brought a championship to our school—and to its coach, Dutch Kleinschmidt. Dutch, the floor is all yours!"

186

The coach rose, laughing. "It's a good thing," he said, "that we're not in training. That food we've just eaten would be enough to slow the team down for a week."

He went on more seriously, to tell of some of the hardships his players had endured and of their courage in adversity. Then he mentioned those who had been injured and praised the substitutes who had done their best to fill their places.

"We can all be glad," he said, "that the injuries weren't worse. In fact, the boys are all here, and I'm going to call on them by name and ask them to stand up. The youngest first—Cal Reagan!"

To a chorus of cheers and clapping the boy got up, his arm in a sling. Then followed Andy Willis, to even louder applause. And finally Flick Davis was called upon.

"Everybody here," said Kleinschmidt, "knows it was Flick who made this team a winner. His good judgment in calling plays, his deadly passing, and most of all his ability to steady the rest of the boys and keep them going—those were all things that helped bring us the championship."

Flick held up his hand to stop the cheering. "That was nice to hear," he told the crowd. "But it was eleven men, pulling together, that really did the job. Like those five big lugs in the middle of the line—like the other backs, who carried the ball an' did the blocking—an' two of the best pass-catching ends in western Kansas! Not only that—this bunch was just as solid on defense as when we had the ball. I'm all through playing at Prairie High, but I'm proud to have been on this team!"

Flick, Tod felt, had just about said it all, and the guests gave him the ovation he deserved. After that the other varsity players were introduced. There were no speeches, but the hearty cheering kept up as man after man got to his feet.

One name after another was mentioned, but Tod didn't hear his own. It worried him a little. Maybe, he thought, Dutch had just forgotten to put him on the list. Finally, after the last member of the scrubs had been introduced, Kleinschmidt held up both hands for silence.

"We're going to miss Flick Davis next season," he said, "but we'll have a new team captain I think you'll all be proud of. Tod Ross—stand up and take a bow!"

Tod got up, his face red with embarrassment. So that, he thought, was what the special football meeting had been about—electing a captain! He didn't try to speak, but the wild applause told him the crowd approved.

When the hubbub died down at last, the master of ceremonies was on his feet again.

"Now," he said, "the Chamber of Commerce is prepared to back up its promises. Remember, we said we'd see that the squad got new uniforms if they won the championship. The coach tells me first-class equipment for thirty men will cost around three thousand dollars. We've already raised an even thousand, and now I'd like to hear some pledges from the floor. Who'll start it off? You, Tim Hoban—two hundred? Good!"

Others followed Mike's father in promising money. The pledges came thick and fast till the total was up to twenty-two hundred dollars. Then only an occasional offer of five or ten dollars was heard.

From a table near the back of the room came Wade Foster's voice. "The head cheerleader," he announced, "says I've got to help the team. Three hundred dollars!"

While the crowd laughed, Tod was figuring. It had reached a bit over twenty-five hundred now, and it looked as if that was all they'd get. He thought of the check in his pocket, and suddenly he found himself standing up.

"Early in the season," he was saying loudly, "I got my nose busted because our old helmets didn't have face guards. So this new equipment means a lot to me. I'd like to pledge five hundred dollars."

For a moment the audience was too stunned to applaud.

188

Then the master of ceremonies got up once more. "Tod," he said, "that was a generous thing to do. But we all wish you'd cut your gift down to—say fifty or a hundred. The rest of us older men can make up what's needed, and I can tell you there'll be face masks on those helmets! How about it, folks? Let me hear some more pledges!"

The response was startling. In no time at all, the total was over the three thousand mark.

The boys at his table stared at Tod in wonder. "Man, you sure did stir 'em up!" said Mike. "Would you really have given the whole five hundred?"

Tod nodded. "I reckon so," he replied. "I thought o' that reward money an' sort o' got carried away."

Mary Ann had taken off her apron and come to the front of the room. She led them all in singing the football fight song, "Ride, Cowboys, Ride!" Then, after the more solemn Prairie Alma Mater, the party was over.

Tod thanked his various committee chairmen for their good work. When he came to Mary Ann, he was a little more personal and took more time.

"Folks won't forget this dinner," he told her. "You girls sure did a job! Where'd you get that roast beef?"

The question made her laugh. "Don't you recognize your own beef when you taste it?" she asked. "Your dad donated every pound of it—a whole prime steer!"

She hesitated and blushed. "I was proud of you tonight, Tod," she said. "Not just because you made that offer, but the way you ran the arrangements. I think you'll make a wonderful captain next year! Good night—see you in history!"

Tod found his father already in the Buick. He waved to some of his departing teammates and took the wheel.

"Whew!" he said. "I'm glad it's all over, but it was quite a night!"

Jim Ross nodded. "Yep," he said. "Good grub—good

folks—and a good cause. I was pretty happy when I finally heard 'em call your name an' found why they'd saved you till the last. Sort o' glad you made the team, boy?"

"That's right, Pa. I'm more than glad. It's great working with a bunch of guys like the Prairie Cowboys!"